MY LiFe

as a

Skysurfing
Skateboarder

BOOKS BY BILL MYERS

The Incredible Worlds of Wally McDoogle (21 books):

—*My Life As a Smashed Burrito with Extra Hot Sauce*
—*My Life As Alien Monster Bait*
—*My Life As a Broken Bungee Cord*
—*My Life As Crocodile Junk Food*
—*My Life As Dinosaur Dental Floss*
—*My Life As a Torpedo Test Target*
—*My Life As a Human Hockey Puck*
—*My Life As an Afterthought Astronaut*
—*My Life As Reindeer Road Kill*
—*My Life As a Toasted Time Traveler*
—*My Life As Polluted Pond Scum*
—*My Life As a Bigfoot Breath Mint*
—*My Life As a Blundering Ballerina*
—*My Life As a Screaming Skydiver*
—*My Life As a Human Hairball*
—*My Life As a Walrus Whoopee Cushion*
—*My Life As a Mixed-Up Millennium Bug*
—*My Life As a Beat-Up Basketball Backboard*
—*My Life As a Cowboy Cowpie*
—*My Life As Invisible Intestines with Intense Indigestion*
—*My Life As a Skysurfing Skateboarder*

Other Series

McGee and Me! (12 books)
Bloodhounds, Inc. (12 books)
Forbidden Doors (12 books)
Secret Agent Dingledorf and His Trusty Dog, Splat

Teen Nonfiction
Hot Topics, Tough Questions
Faith Encounter
Just Believe It

Picture Book
Baseball for Breakfast

www.Billmyers.com

the incredible worlds of **Wally McDoogle**

MY LiFe
as a
Skysurfing Skateboarder

BILL MYERS

Tommy NELSON

www.tommynelson.com

A Division of Thomas Nelson, Inc.
www.ThomasNelson.com

Published in Nashville, Tennessee, by Tommy Nelson®, a Division of Thomas Nelson, Inc. Visit us on the Web at www.tommynelson.com.

Scripture quotations marked (NIV) are from the Holy Bible, New International Version. Copyright © 1973, 1978, 1984 International Bible Society. Used by permission of Zondervan Bible Publishers.

Library of Congress Cataloging-in-Publication Data

Myers, Bill, 1953–
    My life as a sky surfing skateboarder / Bill Myers.
        p. cm — (The incredible worlds of Wally McDoogle ; #21)
    Summary: Wally's disaster-ridden preparation for a skateboarding championship, his Little Buddy's entry in a model car derby race, and his work on his latest superhero story combine to teach Wally a lesson about winning.
    ISBN 0-8499-5992-6
    [1. Winning and losing—Fiction. 2. Skateboarding—Fiction. 3. Christian life—Fiction. 4. Humorous stories.] I. Title.

PZ7.M98234 Mykt 2002
[Fic]—dc21   2002067779

Printed in the United States of America

03 04 05 06 PHX 5 4 3

For: The ISI guys
who know the real race
and how to win it.

But many who are first will be last,
and many who are last will be first.

—Matthew 19:30 (NIV)

Contents

Chapter 1

Just for Starters . . .

Can you believe it? Me, starring in a sports book?

Me, who sprains his wrists tying his shoes?

Me, who breaks into a sweat after a grueling workout with the channel selector?

Me, who . . . well, you get the picture. Yeah, I know there was that book *My Life As a Human Hockey Puck*, but being a human hockey puck is a lot different from competing for the Cross-Country Skateboard Championship of the Universe . . . and a lot less painful.

My story started off innocently enough (don't they all). Just me, my best friend Opera, the human eating machine, and little Leroy (a kid I signed up to be a Big Buddy to). The Big Buddy program is pretty cool. You hang out with some little guy and become like his role model. (Don't worry, I explained to Leroy to ignore the role model part.)

What is cool, though, is that you take them to

all kinds of stuff they wouldn't normally get to go to . . . like the trial races for the Cross-Country Skateboard Championship. On this day, kids all around the country were competing in similar races to qualify for the final, big event the next week.

So, there we were, just me, Opera, Leroy, and—

"Hey, McLoser! You taking notes?"

I looked up to see Bruno the Bruiser shouting at me as he skated past. He was doing his warmup lap, as everyone was fighting for position to start the race.

"Hey, Bruno!" I waved.

"Shut up and get to writing!"

Good ol' Bruno. As you can see, we have a very special relationship: Whenever he needs someone to beat up, I'm the guy. There are other cool benefits, too . . . like giving him my lunch money every day (it's such a bother having to carry it around), or washing his car (he's flunked seventh grade so many times he's old enough to drive . . . and to vote). And, best of all, I get to write his English papers for him.

His current assignment was to write a paper called "My Greatest Hero." And, since he wanted to write it about the world's greatest skateboarder . . . and, since he figured it had to be him (he's not exactly a humble guy), he strongly suggested that I come and watch him skate. (Suggested as in, "If you don't come, McDoogle, you'll be enjoying a lengthy amount of pain during the rest of your very short life.")

So, there I was, standing with Opera, Leroy, and—

"Go, Brunnie . . . Go! Go! Go!"

Oh, yeah, there was also Bruno's dad, Mr. Bruiser—the only person more pushy and bossy than his baby boy.

"Get into position!
Cut off that jerk!
Go! Go! Go! GOOOOOOO . . . !"
(See what I mean?)

Not that Mr. Bruiser didn't have reason to be pushy. In order to get into next week's final race, Bruno had to place as one of the top three in this one. And the competition was tough. In fact, even as he approached the starting line, two very famous skaters were closing in.

Bonnie the Brain—who always used her genius to figure out some new way to go faster. This race she'd greased her body in fish oil to cut down the air friction. (A cool idea except for the stink and the 1,324 cats chasing after her.)

Slacker Sam—the world's greatest cheater. Last year he was so good (or bad) that as soon as they started, he sneaked into a limo, had a seven-course dinner, then was dropped off at the finish line three hours and twenty-two minutes before anyone else. (He almost pulled it off except for the Grey Poupon and hot fudge sauce the judges found spilled on the front of his tuxedo.)

Of course, there were other, not so hot, racers . . . like the kid who was so bad that he took the curve in front of us too high and went shooting off the course.

No problem except that when he shot off the course, he shot right into

K-rash!
("oaff!")

me.

Even that wouldn't have been so bad if he hadn't accidentally slipped off the skateboard and I hadn't accidentally

K-slipped
("uh-oh")

on.

But I could have lived with that if the board hadn't hit the curb, done a 180, shot back onto the track, and caused me to suddenly

Roll, roll, roll, roll . . .
("AUGH!")

join the race.

So, there I was, accidentally racing toward the starting line, doing what I do best . . . hanging on for dear life and screaming my head off. Of course, I wanted to jump off the board, but noticing the ground racing by at a thousand miles per hour, I decided I wasn't in the mood for suicide.

Bruno heard me scream and looked over his shoulder at me. "McDoofus!" he shouted. "What are you doing?!"

I wanted to answer, but it's hard to talk when you're busy passing out from fear.

Anyway, as I reached the starting line, the judge gave the green flag, and the race began.

Bruno, Bonnie, Sam, yours truly, and a half-dozen others flew down Main Street's steep hill. Well, everyone else flew. I just sort of kneeled down, grabbed the side of the board, and prayed my heart out.

The good news was, I managed to travel all the way to the end of the street. The bad news was, I traveled all the way on the *wrong* side of the

"Look out!"
Honk! Honk! Honk!
K-Screech
K-Rash

street.

I knew I should stick around and exchange phone numbers and funeral homes, but suddenly I ran out of street, popped up onto the sidewalk, and headed straight toward the city park with the rest of the racers.

Ah, yes, the park. Now things got kinda interesting . . .

First we were to turn and circle around the giant fountain. A good idea if you know how to turn. Not so good if you don't. For everyone else it was an easy

Swish!
roll, roll, roll.

For me it was a rather hard

Splash!
glug . . . glug . . . glug.

Next up was the giant stairway leading to the lower level. The seasoned pros popped up on the handrails and easily slid down them on the flat of their boards. I chose the stairs, which meant my wheels managed to hit every step-ep-ep-ep a-long-ong-ong-ong-ong the way-ay-ay-ay-ay.

Talk about getting shook up. But at least I was in last place (which is almost as good as being in no place). Unfortunately, the fun and games weren't quite over.

After the steps came the playground obstacle course. Swings, slides, teetertotters . . . You name it, they missed it. They missed it, I

K-Bamb

hit it.

Except for the teetertotters. Somehow I managed to miss the free dental work offered by those face-breakers. Instead, I hit a kid on a tricycle, flipped into the air, and landed smack-dab on one of the seats. Normally, this would have been a good thing, except for the three-thousand-pound sumo wrestler baby who thought slamming down on the other end would be great fun. It was, too, if you happen to like

"AUGHHHH . . ."

sailing high into the air. (Which I didn't.)

The view was pretty good, though. Especially the part where I was flying over everyone else in the race. Yes sir, I could see all my old pals down below. There was Bonnie the Brain and her 1,318 cats (she lost six to some kid with a couple of extra tuna fish sandwiches), Slacker Sam and his nuclear-powered skateboard (I told you the guy knew how to cheat), and in the lead, just below me, Bruno the Bruiser.

It was cool looking down and keeping an eye on my old buddy. It would have been cooler, if I wasn't coming straight down on top of his head.

"Look out!" I screamed. "Look out!!"

Bruiser Boy saw nothing.

"Up here!" I shouted.

He tilted back his head and spotted me. "McDorkle, what are you—

K-Slam

mueing?" (That last word was supposed to be "doing," but it's hard to talk when a part-time author and full-time klutz has just smashed into your face.)

"McMmoooodle! McMmoooodle!"

It was good that he broke my fall (not so good that he'd later be breaking my body). Although I was happy for the free lift he was giving me toward the finish line, I would have been happier if he could see where he was going.

"McMmoooodle! McMmoooodle!"

But there was no way I was getting down off his face. No sir. It was nice and safe up there. Well, except for the approaching train crossing and Bruno Boy's inability to see the upcoming

TOOOOOT . . . TOOOOOT!

Do I even have to say it?

The good news is, we zoomed across the tracks, and the front of the train missed our bodies by just inches. The bad news is, it didn't miss my coat. Suddenly, the locomotive snagged my jacket, and we were flying alongside it at just under a gazillion miles per hour.

"McMmoooodle! Mhat's moing mon? Mhat's moing mon?"

I wanted to tell him, but I knew my free ride would be over if my chauffeur suddenly had a heart attack. So, I tried to be positive and look on the bright side. "You know that math test we're supposed to have on Monday?" I shouted.

"Messss," he yelled.

"Well, it looks like we won't be taking it . . . or any other test ever again!" (Unless there's an entrance exam to get into heaven.)

Something about the way he screamed told me he wasn't thrilled with the idea. But that was okay because I looked up and saw the finish line approaching. "We're almost there!" I shouted. "We're almost there!"

With a little wiggling and a ton of tugging, I finally pulled my jacket loose. Now we were free of the locomotive and barreled toward the finish line under our own power . . . well, except for the few hundred miles per hour of speed we'd picked up from the little choo-choo.

The good news was, we crossed the finish line in record time. The bad news was, someone had built a department store directly across the street from that finish line. A department store with one very large

K-rash
tinkle, tinkle, tinkle

picture window, and one very hard

K-Smash
(Anyone got an aspirin?)

wall at the other end.

But at last it was over; we had finally stopped. And, other than the trip the hospital to set a few broken bones and replace a few missing organs, Bruno had qualified for the upcoming race, and I had managed to survive another misadventure.

Unfortunately, this little misadventure was simply a warmup for something bigger and, as usual, a whole lot more painful.

Chapter 2

Wally McDoogle, Superstar!

I'd barely dragged my bruised and battered body through the front door before one of my older brothers, Burt (or was it Brock? I can never keep those twins straight) glanced up from the TV and greeted me. "Congratulations, bud."

I stopped cold. Who was he talking to?

"Saw you on the news," he said.

I looked around. Nobody else was there. Just me. Could it be? Was it possible? Taking the chance that he was actually speaking to me like a human being, I ventured an answer and said, "Yeah?"

"Yeah. They say you tied for first place with that Bruno guy. Nice work."

My heart pounded in my chest. I couldn't catch my breath. I was feeling faint. Not only had my brother talked to me, but it almost sounded like, could it be, YES! He had actually given me a compliment!!

Not believing my ears and thinking it was some kind of dream, I gasped, "Me? Are you talking to me?"

"Who else, Moron."

Well, at least I knew it wasn't a dream. And to prove the point, he finished with an ever-so-thoughtful request. "Now quit stinking up the room and get out of here."

Yes sir, it had been for real. Imagine, an actual compliment from an older brother. Unbelievable. I headed for my room, sort of floating up the stairs. (Well, except for the part where I tripped over our cat, Collision, who, as you may remember, did not get her name by accident.) After scraping myself from the bottom of the stairs and heading up them a second time

"MEOW!"
stumble, stumble, K-Rash!

—er, make that a third time—I finally got to my bedroom.

I opened the door just as the phone was ringing. I grabbed it and answered, "Hello?"

"Hey, Wally." It was Wall Street, my other best friend, even though she is a girl.

"What's up?" I asked.

"I've been on the phone all afternoon."

"Buying more stocks and bonds?" I asked.

"Better than that. I just talked to Buford K. Flabbyjowls, president of Sizzlin' Skateboards."

"That's nice," I said as I hopped onto my bed and

K-boing!
"AUGH!"
K-thud!

bounced onto the floor. (Ever have one of those days? Unfortunately, I have one of those lives.)

"And you know who we were talking about?" she asked.

"Who?" I said, after regaining consciousness.

"You."

Suddenly, fear filled my heart. You see, Wall Street loves money. In fact, she plans to make her first million by the time she's fourteen. Unfortunately, most of the money she's made so far has all been made off me.

Knowing better, but unable to help myself, I asked the most dangerous question in the world. At least the most dangerous question when it comes to Wall Street's wallet and my well-being: "What do you want from me?"

"I told him all about your performance at today's race."

I didn't like the sound of her voice. "And?" I asked nervously.

"And, if we're lucky, he may sponsor us in next Saturday's cross-country championship!"

"What are you talking about?" I asked.

"You qualified, didn't you?"

"Yeah, but it was an accident. I can't skate."

"So?"

"So, don't you think skating might come in handy during the race?"

"Why do you always get hung up on details?" she sighed. "The point is, he can make us a ton of money in a real short time."

"Us?" I gulped.

"Sure, I'm your agent, now."

"But—"

"Just leave everything to me."

"But, but—"

"Show up Monday at his office, three-thirty sharp."

"But, but, but—"

"Oh, and Wally?"

"Yeah?"

"When you get there, try not to do anything stupid—you know, like tripping over his desk or burning the place down."

I took another nervous gulp.

"Wally?"

"All right," I sighed. "But no promises."

"Cool. I'll see you at three-thirty sharp. And if he likes you, he'll call in his personal trainer to give you a few tips. See ya." With that, she hung up.

So did I. But even now, I knew I'd better talk Dad into increasing my medical coverage . . . and my life insurance.

I managed to crawl into bed, snap off the light, and snap on Ol' Betsy, my laptop computer. Needless to say, I was more than a little tense over Monday's meeting. And the best way to relax was to start up another one of my superhero stories.

It has been another incredibly good day of generosity from our graciously generous and gorgeously good-looking good guy—Kid Giver. Already he has given nine gallons of blood to the Red Cross, or was it ten (don't worry, he takes vitamins), and emptied his closet and given all of his clothes (and his mom's) to the Salvation Army (don't

worry, she loves to shop). And now,
at this precise moment, he is fin-
ishing his seventy-two hours of vol-
unteer work at the homeless shelter
soup kitchen. He is just plopping a
glop of something on some guy's food
tray that looks like a cross between
prechewed lima beans and a pound of
pond sludge (hey, he just serves the
stuff, he doesn't cook it) when suddenly his

Giv-ring... Giv-ring

Generosity Phone rings.
   He pulls the phone from his pocket
and answers:

"Hi, there....
Giving is greater
than being a taker."
(Okay, so he's no poet.)

A woman's voice gasps on the other
end, "Kid Giver... is that you?"
   "Mom? Are you all right? Look, I'm
sorry about those clothes, but——"
   "I've got worse news than that."

"What is it, Mom? An earthquake in India? More people starving in Ethiopia? The church needs a new parking lot?"

"No, Kid, it's worse than any of those."

"What could be worse than people suffering, starving, or needing a fancier place to park their BMWs?"

"It's worse than all those worses put together."

"No," our hero gasps a heroic gasp. "You don't mean..."

"Yes!" she cries. "It's your evil twin brother...

Ta-da-daaaaa...
(If you don't know what
that is, you're obviously not
reading enough of these books.)

...Greedy Guy."

"Oh, no!" our hero shouts. "Don't tell me he's escaped from the Prison of the Sinfully Selfish?"

"Okay."

"So, what happened?"

"I can't tell you," she says.

"Why not?!"

"You told me not to."

"Oh, no!" our hero cries. "Don't tell me he REALLY has escaped from the Prison of the Sinfully Selfish?"

"Okay..."

"So, what happened?"

"I can't tell you," she says.

"Why not?!"

"Dear, haven't we already had this discussion?"

"Oh, no!"

"Oh, yes!"

"Oh, no!"

"Sweetheart, shouldn't we get on with the story?"

"You're right!" he cries. "So, how do you know he's escaped?"

"He just called me—collect, of course—and..."

greeeeeeeed...

"Mom, what's that sound?"

"That's what I've been trying to tell you." Her voice is growing weaker. "Your brother has just invented a Sonic Greed Generator."

"A what?"

"He is playing it over every radio and TV station in the country to control our minds."

"Oh, no!"

"Oh, yes!"

"Oh, no!"

"Dear, let's move along now." Her voice grows fainter. "So far I've been able to...fight off its power...but...now..."

"Mom, are you there? Mom, can you hear me?"

At last her voice comes back, but it is flat and lifeless: "Buy me a DVD player."

"Mom——"

"And give me your house."

"Mom——"

"And sign your bank account over to me. Oh, and let me have all the loose change in your pocket."

"Mom, this doesn't sound like you at all. It sounds more like..."

Ta-Ta-Daaaa...
(That, of course, is hero
realization music——which,
of course, is slightly different

from the bad-guy music
you've already heard.)

    Because, although he's not the
brightest candle on the cake, our
hero does finally manage to catch on.

    "Mom, are you falling under the
Greed Generator's power?"

    "I can't tell you."

    "Why not?"

    "It would mean giving you informa-
tion."

    "So?"

    "So, I can no longer give any-
thing."

    "Hey, get off that phone!" the
homeless man in the food line shouts.
"And give me more of that lima bean
and pond sludge!"

    Startled, Kid Giver looks up, then
stares at the green gunk in his serv-
ing spoon. "You're kidding, right?"

    "I want it all!" the guy growls.

    "And I want more of that kitty
litter!" the person in front of him
shouts, pointing at the pan of over-
cooked peas.

    "No!" the cook shouts as he appears.

He wraps one arm around the pan of
kitty litt——I mean, peas——and the other
around the lima gruel. "You can't have
them. They're mine, all mine!"

"But"——Kid frowns at him——"you made
it for them."

"It doesn't matter; it's mine,
now. All mine!"

Unfortunately, it's not just the
cook or the people in line who are
turning selfish. All around the room
people are shouting and grabbing
things. One person is hoarding chairs.
Another is collecting all the dirty
food trays. One guy's even scraping
the dirt from people's shoes and
screaming, "Mine! Mine, mine, mine!"

Desperately, our hero looks about
the room until he spots the
reason...it's the TV in the far cor-
ner. Ever so faintly, from the
speaker, he hears a high-pitched

greeeeeeeeed...

"What on earth could that be?" he
wonders (hey, I told you he wasn't the
brightest candle), until he suddenly

realizes, "Of course, that's what's putting everyone under its spell." (Okay, so he's no Sherlock Holmes, either.) "That's what's filling everyone with greed. That's why everyone's going crazy, grabbing and fighting like shoppers at the mall just before Christmas." (Well, not quite that bad—but you get the idea.)

Then, just as our hero understands the truth, he also starts to fall under the Greed Generator's spell. He begins eyeing the rags on the homeless man's back, checking out the wadded napkins in the trash bin, the dust bunnies in the corners, when suddenly—

RING . . . RING . . .

I glanced up from Ol' Betsy. My story was just starting to get interesting and someone was calling. With a heavy sigh I picked up the phone and answered, "Hello . . ."

"Hey . . . *crunch, crunch.*"

"Hi, Opera," I said. "What's up?"

"How'd, *munch, munch,* you know it was me?"

"Lucky guess. What's going on?"

"You kinda deserted Leroy this afternoon. So I, *crunch, munch,* took him back home."

"Oh, thanks."

"Don't, *burp,* mention it. He just wanted to make sure that, *belch,* you were still taking him to the Big Buddy model car derby next Saturday."

"Listen, Opera, I kinda got a lot on my mind right now. Can we talk about this later?"

"No problem. I'm kinda busy, too. I still got to eat three more bags of these Chippy Chipper potato chips, *BURP (Wow, that was a good one!),* to make my daily quota before I go to bed." (Hey, everyone needs a goal.) "I'll catch you Monday after school."

"Great," I said.

"*Belch,*" he agreed.

But even as I hung up I knew Opera and Leroy would be the last things on my mind . . .

. . . especially Monday after school . . .

. . . especially at Sizzlin' Skateboards. . . .

Chapter 3

First Impressions

When we arrived at the Sizzlin' Skateboards office, I was on my best behavior—no falling down and cracking open my head in the lobby, no tumbling down the escalators. I even managed to shake the secretary's hand without breaking it (or mine).

Unfortunately, I also managed to use up my entire quota of coordination for the day, *before* we even met Buford K. Flabbyjowls. So, when he opened his office door to greet Wall Street and me, I knew anything could (and probably would) happen. Of course, it all started off smoothly enough . . .

"Hey, Dudes," he said, reaching up and giving us a high-five. "Come on in, and let's hang for a while."

Wall Street and I traded looks. It's not every

day you hear some sixty-year-old guy (with at least that many double chins) speaking in 'surferese.' Even stranger was the way he was all dressed up in a helmet, knee pads, elbow pads, hip pads, and wrist protectors.

Seeing the expression on our faces he asked, "S'up?"

Wall Street smiled. "Uh, nothing."

He suddenly broke out laughing, which sent ripples across all the flab in his body. He motioned to his protective gear and said, "I just thought I should be prepared."

"Prepared?" Wall Street asked.

He nodded as he waddled into his office. As we followed him in, he explained, "I was just surfin' the Net and gettin', like, the four-one-one on our bud here."

"You mean Wally?" Wall Street asked. "You were checking up on Wally?"

"Well, that's one name," Flabbyjowls said as he sat behind his desk, which looked like a giant skateboard. "But this dude, he, like, goes by a few others, too." He clicked the computer in front of him and read from the screen: "'Wally the Walking Disaster Area,' 'Wally the All-School Punching Bag,' and, oh, here's one that, like, I totally don't get . . . 'Wally the Human Swirlee'?"

"Oh, that," I explained, only too happy to help. "A swirlee is where the older kids turn you upside down and stick your head in the toilet and flush it."

He looked up and asked doubtfully, "And you, like, totally get into this?"

I shrugged. "Everyone needs a hobby."

"Pretty gnarly, Dude." He shook his head from left to right . . . while the flab in his neck took a moment to catch up, making it go from right to left. Amazing. It was like watching two tennis matches at the same time. Even after he stopped shaking his head, his neck kept going back and forth, like a giant bowl of Jell-O.

"Is that why you're wearing all that protective gear?" Wall Street asked. "'Cause you're afraid something might happen to you?"

He nodded up and down, which, of course, made his neck flab bob down and up. He motioned for us to sit in the chairs across from his desk.

And then it happened . . .

Hey, it wasn't my fault that the chair wasn't where I thought it was.

And you can't blame me for grabbing the desk when I started to fall.

And it wasn't my fault that I accidentally

grabbed the blotter on the desk instead,
. . . which had the cup of hot coffee on it
. . . which spilled onto Flabbyjowls's lap
. . . which made him leap higher than Michael Jordan on a pogo stick

"YEOW!"

. . . which sent his chair rolling backward into the bookcase
. . . which teetered back and forth, and forth and back
. . . which probably wasn't going to fall until I raced over to stop it
. . . which caused me to trip over the umbrella stand, screaming,

"This isn't going so well, is it . . ."

. . . as I stumbled into Mr. Flabbyjowls's arms
. . . which caused us to fall back into his chair
. . . which shot across the room at a gazillion and a half miles per hour
. . . which hit the plate-glass window
. . . which shattered as we flew through it, with me yelling, . . .

"AUGH!"

and him yelling,

"Totally Outrageous, Dude!"

. . . until we

K-Thud

hit the sidewalk two stories below. Well, Mr. Flabbyjowls hit the sidewalk two stories below. I sort of

K-squish

hit Mr. Flabbyjowls, which, if you remember that bowl of Jell-O we talked about earlier, really wasn't all that painful.

Yes sir, it was definitely one of my better disasters, rating about an 8.7 on the McDoogle Catastrophe Scale.

And I wasn't the only one impressed. When Mr. Flabbyjowls finally regained consciousness, he looked up at me in fear and amazement. Then, shaking his head, he muttered, "Awesome, Dude. Totally awesome," before dropping back into a rather deep and somewhat lengthy coma.

* * * * *

"Mezter Flabbyjowlz, Mezter Flabbyjowlz!"

The paramedics were just loading him into the ambulance when this musclebound jock (complete with a sixty-five-inch chest and an IQ to match) came racing at us.

"Mezter Flabbyjowlz, Mezter Flabbyjowlz! Are yoo all right?" (Hey, what good is it having a musclebound jock, if he doesn't sound like Arnold Schwarzenegger?)

Of course, Mr. Flabbyjowls did not answer. (That's one of the drawbacks of being unconscious.) But the way his fat jiggled up and down with each move of the paramedics, it looked like he was nodding.

"Vhere are zey taking yoo?"

"To the hospital," I said.

Muscle Man looked over at me, then back at Flabbyjowls. "Iz zez hem?" he asked, pointing at me. "Iz zez ze new zkateboard zenzation?"

Again Flabbyjowls's body jiggled, and again it looked like he nodded.

Muscle Mind frowned at me, then looked back at Mr. Flabbyjowls. "Are yoo zure?"

Another jiggle, another nod.

Then, as they finished pushing him into the ambulance, Muscle Guy called after him, "Vell, don't yoo vorry, Mezter Flabbyjowlz—I vill get hem in zhape vor next veek'z raze! I vill make zure he vins ze championzhip!"

They shut the ambulance's back doors and headed for the front.

"I don't know how," Muscle Guy muttered as he looked down at me in disgust, "but I vill."

As the siren kicked on and the ambulance took off, I figured now was as good a time as any to set the guy straight. Unfortunately, Wall Street wasn't figuring the same figure I was figuring (go figure).

I started to explain. "Listen, I'm not—"

"What he means," Wall Street suddenly stepped in, "is that he's not in that bad of shape."

Muscle Mutant looked at me doubtfully. "I haf never zeen a perzon zo zkinnee."

"Yeah, I know," I shrugged. "But it comes in handy when they need someone to get balls out of downspouts."

"And vhat about taking showerz? Aren't yoo avraid ov getting zucked down ze drain?"

Before I could answer, he suddenly reached out his arm and wrapped his fingers around my chest (yeah, unfortunately, you read that right: "*fingers* around *chest*"). Then, he picked me up and said, "Come! Ve hafn't mooch time."

It was a short jog to the gym—at least for

him. But Wall Street had to run for all she was worth just to keep up. While I, on the other hand, simply stayed in his grip (not that I had much choice). It was a definite King Kong moment, being carried through the streets in this big guy's monster hand. But at least I wasn't screaming my head off in fear like the girl in those movies— then again, it's hard to scream your head off in fear when you've passed out.

"Ah." He grinned as we finally slowed to a stop. "Ere ve are."

I looked up to read the name. "Mold's Gym?" I asked.

"Yes." He nodded as he stepped inside. "Ere ve vill train yoo to be a man, to become a vorld champion, to—"

"—make more money than we ever dreamed possible," Wall Street panted, as she staggered in from behind.

"Great," I gulped, looking around at all the workout equipment. "Just great."

Unfortunately, we wasted little time. Before I could call 911 they had me running on the treadmill. It was brutal, it was exhausting . . . it was even worse when they finally turned it on.

"AUGH!"
thud, thud, thud, thud

"AUGH!"
thud, thud, thud, thud

For those of you new to the pain part of
these novels, the "AUGH!" is the sound of one
Wally McDoogle falling down on the treadmill.
While the *thud, thud, thud, thud* is the sound of
one Wally McDoogle getting his foot stuck on
the belt and being dragged under the machine
until he comes back up at the front where we
get to start the whole process

"AUGH!"
thud, thud, thud, thud

over again.
"Come, Vally, yoo muzt try harder!"
"I'm—

"AUGH!"
thud, thud, thud, thud

trying! I'm trying!"
"Vizualize yoor goal. Zen run to it . . . run to
it like ze vind!"
"Can't I just—

"AUGH!"

thud, thud, thud, thud

take a taxi?"

After destroying my lower body for a few hours, we focused upon some upper-body destruction. Translation: I began lifting weights. So, there I was, on my back gripping the bar, pushing and straining against it for all I was worth.

"EEEE ERRRRR AHHHHH!"

Wall Street stayed in the room, urging me on, doing her best imitation of a cheerleader:

"Wally, Wally, he's our man,
If he can't do it, anyone can!"

I'm not entirely convinced she had the words right. (Then again, maybe they were righter than I thought.)

Anyway, working out in the weight room was full of sweat and pain and tears. It got even more painful when they actually started putting weights on the bar.

And last, but certainly not least, came the sit-ups. How long we did these, I don't remember. I do remember the sweat pouring off my face as the minutes slowly ticked away . . . as one hour turned to two, then to three, until finally, with Wall Street pushing and Mr. Musclez pulling, I finally succeeded in completing my very first sit-up.

(Hey, I'm a writer, not an athlete.)

The success was overwhelming. It touched us all very deeply. Especially Mr. Musclez (giant tears streamed down his face). "I've never zeen anyzing zo pazetic," he cried. "Yoo'll never be ready en zuch a zort time. Yoo'll never be ready."

(I didn't have the heart to tell him that the problem was not the short amount of time . . . but the short amount of athletic ability of Vally McDoogle.)

Still, all good things must come to an end, no matter how painful. Eventually, they scraped me off the mat and carried me home. All the time they kept saying, "Tomorrow's a new day, tomorrow's a new day," while all the time I kept praying, "Please, God, end the world tonight, end the world tonight."

And yet, even then, despite the pain and humiliation, a part of me was beginning to like this competition business. I mean, if I really bore down, if I really practiced, maybe I could beat Bonnie the Brain, or Slacker Sam, or maybe even Bruno the Bruiser. After all, I beat them in the elimination race, didn't I? Imagine, with all my other titles, being able to add "Wally McDoogle, Skateboard Champion of the World."

Of course, my chances were next to impossible, but if I put my mind to it, if I didn't let anything get in my way (including dying from these workout sessions) . . . maybe, just maybe I really could reach that dream.

But, unfortunately, as we all know, my dreams usually turn into nightmares.

Chapter 4

Priorities

So, there I was, dragging into my house, with dreams of becoming a champion skateboarder staggering through my head. (They would have been dancing through my head, but at the moment, they were as tired as I was.)

"Hey, Moron."

I turned and saw—who else?—but my older brother Brock (or was it Burt?). He was sitting in front of the TV as if he hadn't moved since last night. Maybe he hadn't. As a leading expert in couch potato-ing, he knew all the moves (or nonmoves)—tricks of the trade like begging Mom to bring in his meals, like telling Dad he's allergic to going out and getting a summer job. And going to the bathroom? I wasn't sure how he pulled that off, though I do remember seeing a garden hose stretching from the sofa all the way into the bathroom.

Repeat after me: *EEWwww* . . . (Very good.)

"What's up?" I asked him as I stumbled into the room.

He popped open a can of soda and, being the polite guy he is, guzzled down its entire contents before sighing in contentment, "Ahhh . . . *Belch*." Finally, he answered. "Your buddy is upstairs waiting for you."

"Which one?" I asked.

He gave me one of those who-are-you-kidding looks—which I totally deserved since my list of friends is a bit on the short side. First, there's Wall Street and Opera, then Opera and Wall Street, then Wall Street and . . . well, you get the picture. We are all members of Dorkoids Anonymous, a club that hasn't gained any new members since we formed it and voted me president.

"Thanks," I said to Brock (or was it Burt?) as I started for the stairs.

"Uh, Wally?"

"Yeah?"

"You want to hand me that garden hose over there?"

I ran up the stairs as quickly as possible. As I headed down the hall toward my room, I could already tell who was waiting for me. Something about the smell of greasy potato chips and the perpetual *munch-munch-munch*ing from behind my door was a good clue.

"Hey, Opera," I said as I pushed it open.

He was sitting on the floor, crunching away. "How'd you, *burp,* know it was me?"

"Lucky guess," I said.

But Opera wasn't my only visitor. Because, sitting beside him was . . .

"Hey, Leroy." I grinned. "What brings you here?"

Instead of answering, the little guy leaped up and raced over to give me a giant hug. "Wally . . ."

It was a touching moment, though it would have been a bit more touching without all my bruised muscles and broken bones from the workout. Still, I was able to return the hug and give him the mandatory hair tousle. "What's up?" I asked.

And then I saw it—wood, nails, screws, and glue—scattered all over my floor. "What are you guys doing?" I asked.

"Saturday is the model car derby race," Opera belched.

"So?"

"And since you need to build a model car to enter the derby, and since you've been too busy, I figured I'd help you and Leroy get started."

Good ol' Opera, always looking out for the

next guy. But the place was a disaster area—
worse than Mom's bathroom after she spends
all morning getting ready for church. Well,
maybe not that bad, but close. And there, in the
center of the mess, was the weirdest contrap-
tion I'd ever seen.

"What on earth?" I asked as I stooped down
to examine something that looked like a cross
between an old tennis shoe and a pipe organ. I
knew it was supposed to be a model car for the
derby, but it was impossible to tell . . . except for
the seven or eight wheels that stuck out at different angles.

"What do you think?" Opera asked proudly.

I laughed. "That's the stupidest thing I've
ever seen."

"Wally—"

"No offense," I said with a chuckle, "but it is so
ignorant they'll laugh you right out of the race."

"Wally—"

"Come on, Opera," I said. "You're only good
at two things . . . eating and, well, eating, so—"

"Which is why I let *Leroy* do all the building!" Opera blurted.

Oops. Talk about feeling stupid. I slowly
turned to Leroy . . . his lower lip trembling like
jelly on a jackhammer, his eyes already filling
with tears.

"Hey," I said, trying to make him feel better. "It's not that bad."

He nodded and gave his little eyes a little swipe.

"It's just . . . well, if you want to be a winner, you've got to be better than anyone else. If you want to win, you've got to focus on winning and only winning."

Again his little head nodded.

"And this . . ." I turned to the tennis shoe pipe organ, "this just doesn't cut it, little guy."

"That's why we brought it over here," Opera said. "So you can help."

I let out a heavy sigh. "I'd love to, guys, but I'm really beat. I need to get some sleep."

Little Leroy gave another little sniff. "But the derby is Saturday, and you promised," he said.

It killed me to see my little pal trying not to cry. It was even worse knowing I was the reason. He was right, I *had* promised.

"Oh, okay," I finally said, "but just for a while."

The kid's face lit up.

I continued, "We can work on your model an hour or so tonight, and then a couple of hours every day until—"

ring . . . ring . . .

I scooped up my phone and answered, "Hello?"

"Wally? Wall Street here. I'm going to e-mail you some maps of the skateboard course for you to study tonight."

"Tonight?"

"You can't do it tomorrow; you'll be working out all day."

"Yeah, but . . ." I threw a look over to Opera and Leroy, who waited patiently. "I've got plans."

"Listen," Wall Street said, "do you want to win this thing or not?"

"Of course I do, but—"

"Then you gotta make some sacrifices."

"But Leroy's here and we were—"

"If you want to be a winner, you've got to be better than anyone else. You've got to focus on winning and only winning and not let anything get in your way."

The words sounded vaguely familiar. And, unfortunately, they made sense. I stole another look at Opera.

"Wally?" Wall Street said.

Then to Leroy.

"Wally, do you want to win this thing or not?"

I took a deep breath and slowly let it out. "All right," I sighed. "Go ahead and e-mail them."

"And you'll study them tonight?"

"Yes," I sighed again, "I'll study them tonight."

"Great. I'll see you at the gym at four-thirty tomorrow morning."

"Four-thirty!" I croaked. "In the morning?!"

"Do you want to win?"

"Yes, but—"

"I'll see you at four-thirty then."

"All right."

"See," she said, "you're already thinking like a winner."

"Yeah, right." I slowly hung up the phone and looked across the room. There were Opera and Leroy, looking toward me more than a little sad. From what they heard of the conversation, they already knew what I had to say. "Sorry, guys." I shrugged. "I've got some work to do tonight."

"That's okay," Opera said. He bent down and started picking up the stuff. "We figured as much."

I turned to Leroy. "But we'll work on it to-morrow, okay?"

The little guy forced a little grin. "Okay, Wally," he kinda half-squeaked, "whatever you say."

"I promise," I said.

They both nodded in silence as they continued picking up.

I would have liked to help them clean up, but since Wall Street was e-mailing the map, and since I had no time to spare, I reached over and snapped on the computer.

Of course, it hurt to have to put off Opera and the little guy, but I really didn't have any choice. Like Wall Street said, if I wanted to be a winner, I had to focus. And I couldn't let anything or anyone get in the way.

* * * * *

I'd been studying the route for Saturday's race through our town for hours. It was all mapped out as if we were skating through different parts of the world. I don't want to say it was late, but I probably got to bed a couple of hours after God. I was definitely exhausted in a major point-me-to-the-bed-and-just-let-me-fall-over kind of way. But, once I was in bed, I still couldn't sleep.

I suppose lots of it had to do with what I'd studied. I had no idea that a cross-country skateboard race meant having to actually travel . . . "cross-country." Okay, so I won't be winning any brain prizes, but I didn't know it would actually involve swamps and rivers and mountains . . . all just waiting for the opportunity to break major McDoogle body parts. But that wasn't the only reason I couldn't sleep. The other had to do with Opera and little Leroy. Not only because of what I'd said, but because of what I had to do . . .

As you no doubt noticed, this Saturday was the day of the skateboard race. It was also the day of the model car derby. (And if you hadn't noticed, then you won't be getting any brain prizes, either.) Still, like Wall Street said, if I wanted to be a champion, I couldn't let anything or anyone get in my way. Not even promises to my friends.

So, with that cheery, Benedict Arnold thought rattling through my head, I reached for Ol' Betsy and returned to my superhero story. Yes sir, nothing beats a little writing to help you forget your guilt.

When we last left our supergood guy, the genuinely great and genetically generous Kid Giver was falling under the influence of his twin brother's...

Ta-da-da...

Sonic Greed Generator.

We join him now as he races into the streets, trying to clear his mind of the awful hypnotic tone. But the

greeeeeeeeeeeeed...

sound is all around him. And it's
affecting everyone. Everywhere he
looks folks are becoming greedy. Some
are taking money just for giving
directions, others are taking money
just for giving the time of day. And
don't even ask about all those people
taking each other to court for
breathing each other's air.

Using all of his super willpower
to overcome the tone, our hero leaps
on a park bench and shouts, "People!
People, listen to me!"

But no one hears. They are too
busy scrambling and scratching,
hoarding and collecting, taking
everything they can find, from pocket
lint, to used candy wrappers, to prechewed gum.

Suddenly, he has an idea. "Listen
to me," he shouts. "I'm GIVING you
free advice."

And with that single word, "giving," a
crowd of 1.3 million people immediately

> *run, run, run...*
> *and*
> *surround, surround, surround...*

him.

"Listen!" he shouts. "You must pay attention! You must give me your attention!"

Unfortunately, the words "pay" and "give" cause them to

> *run, run, run...*
> *and*
> *disappear, disappear, disappear...*

even faster.

"No, no, no!" he shouts. "This is for FREE. I'm GIVING you my opinion. You can TAKE my advice."

Immediately, they're

> *run, run, running...*
> *and*
> *elbowing, elbowing, el—*
> *"OW! That's my eye!"*

their way back.

Kid Giver begins to explain. "My

brother is hypnotizing you! With sound waves he is giving you this desire to take. He's giving you feelings of greed and——"

"Giving?!" someone shouts.

"Yes," Kid says. "He is **GIVING** you these feelings over the radio and TV."

"So, why are we wasting time here?" another cries.

Suddenly, the crowd scatters in all directions for their radios and TVs to get even more greed. Well, everyone but this single, solitary kid who stays by our hero's side.

"Mr. Superhero? Mr. Superhero?" The little guy tugs on Kid Giver's coat.

Our hero looks at him and smiles. "Well, one of you is better than none." He sighs.

"You owe me $32.95," the little fellow complains.

"For what?"

"For **GIVING** you my attention."

Our hero frowns. "Are you **GIVING** me a hard time?"

"If I am, it will cost you an additional $12.50."

"Please," Kid Giver mutters, "**GIVE** me a break."

"That will be an extra $7.40."

Then, just before we wear that joke out (as if we haven't already), the Generosity Phone

Giv-rings...Giv-rings.

Kid pulls out the cell phone and answers.

"Hi, there....
Giving is greater
than being a——"

"Yeah, yeah, I read that in the last section——"

"Brother?" Kid Giver cries. "Is that you?"

"I'd say yes, but that would mean **GIVING** you information."

"Please," our hero shouts as he looks at the chaos in the street around him. "We can't go on like this. The world cannot survive if all people do is take."

"What do you want me to do?"

"**GIVE** up."

"Just had to work that in, didn't you? Look, you know how these stories go. I can't turn myself in until we have a big showdown."

"Oh, that's right."

Greedy Guy sighs. "Twenty-one books in this series, and he still doesn't know how it works."

"I guess it's because I **GIVE** all my books away before I——"

"Stop using that word!"

"I'm sorry, brother. Please for-**GIVE** me."

"I'm warning you!"

"Are you **GIVING** me an ultimatum?"

"Knock it off!" the bad brother bellows. "Just meet me at my secret hideout in one hour!"

Before Kid Giver can ask for directions, his brother hangs up.

Oh, no, what will Kid Giver do? How will he ever find the hideout? How will he stop his brother from destroying the world with greed? And most important, will we have to put up with any more of those **GIVING** jokes?

These and other major questions fill our good guy's noggin when suddenly—

BUZZZZZZZZZZZ

That, of course, was my alarm clock going off. I glanced up from Ol' Betsy. Great, just great. It was already 4:30 A.M. That meant I didn't get any sleep at all. And if today's workout was anything like yesterday's, I'd need every minute I could get. Then again, if today's workout was anything like yesterday's, I might not need sleep at all. . . .

Since when do dead people need sleep?

Chapter 5

Buckling In and Pumping Up...

The next day's workout was worse than the first. Actually, the pain was about the same (you can't get any more unbearable than unbearable). But it was the company I kept that made it worse. I had Mr. Musclez, my personal trainer:

"Vork, Vally, vork! Yoo cannot haf victory, iv yoo don't haf vork!"

(I wanted to point out that you can't have victory, if you don't have life—but he didn't seem interested in those types of details.)

Then there was Wall Street, my personal cheerleader:

"Let's win that race,
Let's make some dough.
Just laugh at pain,
Just say, 'Ho-ho.'"

(Hey, she's a day-trader, not a poet.)

Unfortunately, her other cheer wasn't much better:

"Money markets,
Stock markets,
Junk bonds . . . Yea!
Invest in them all,
If you live through the day."
(Told you.)

And finally, least but not last, there were Bruno and his dad. They'd been there an hour before we even showed up. And Mr. Bruiser was pushing his son for all he was worth:
"Let's go, Brunnie. Go! Go! Go!"
Eventually, when we were working out side by side, I turned to him. "Bruno?" I wheezed during my finger raises (it would have been leg raises, but I was working my way up to them). "What are you doing here?"
Before Bruno could answer, his dad shouted, "You got the best trainer in the state here, McDorkle. We're going to learn your secrets, and then we're going to use them to crush you in Saturday's big race! Ain't that right, boy?!"

"Yeah"—Bruno nodded, giving a painful gasp—"that's right."

"Let's go, Brunnie. Let's go! Go! Go!"

"Is winning really that important to you?" I asked Bruno.

Again Mr. Bruiser cut him off and shouted, "Winning is everything! Okay, son, give me five thousand push-ups. Let's go! Go! Go!"

Bruno got down on the mat and just before he started, he glanced into my eyes. It was then I saw the real truth. Winning wasn't that important to Bruno. It was only important to him because it was important to his dad. It was like the only way his dad knew how to connect with him—you know, a father-to-son kind of thing.

"Let's go, boy!" his dad hollered. "Let's go! Go! Go!"

"Right," Bruno groaned as he started the push-ups.

Poor kid. At least when I spend quality time with my dad (usually after one of my mishaps), there's no shouting and yelling. Hospital emergency rooms don't allow that sort of thing.

"Vally, come!" Mr. Musclez motioned for me to follow.

"Where are we going now?" I asked as I tried to untangle myself from one of the weightlifting machines.

"Ve're going to a voto zhoot."

"A vhat?" I asked.

"A voto zhoot. It'z vhere zey take picturez ov yoo all pumped up and en action."

"You mean like an action poster?" I asked.

"Yez, exaztly. Zo, vhen zey zee yoo on a Zizzilin' Zkateboard, zey'll vant to buy vone."

"Because?" I asked, fearing the worst.

"Becauze zey vant to be juzt like yoo."

"You sure that's such a good idea?" I asked.

He shook his head. "No, Vally. I zink it'z a louzy idea. But zince zat'z vhat Mezter Flabby-jowlz vanted, and zince he'z ztill in a coma . . ."

I nodded and immediately began praying. Not so much for the photo shoot as for Mr. Flabbyjowls's miraculous recovery . . .

* * * * *

An hour later I was standing in the hot lights of a photo studio, with a photographer, his two burly assistants, Franz and Fritz, and his rather thick Australian accent:

"Aw-right, mate, let's peel off yer shirt and show the camera here what ya got."

"What I've got?" I asked.

"That's right, lad. Let's see them bulging biceps, them terrific triceps, them powerful pec—"

"Uh, I'm not sure what you're talking about," I said.

"I'm talking about yer muscles, mate. Take off yer shirt and show me yer muscles."

"I, uh . . ." I threw a nervous look to Mr. Musclez. "I don't think that's such a good idea."

My trainer stepped forward and agreed. "I em avraid he'z right. Ze zhirt zhould ztay on."

"Don't be daft, mate," the photographer said, reaching over to my shirt and peeling it off. "I'm a professional; I know what sells and what—"

"Augh!" Fritz cried.

"Ugh!" Franz gagged.

"I think I'm going to hurl!" the photographer gasped as he quickly shoved the shirt back at me.

"I tried to warn you," I said.

After regaining his composure, Photo Guy forced a smile and tried again. "Not to worry, mate. We'll just shoot ya from the legs down and—"

Again I shook my head.

"Another bad idea?" he asked.

I nodded.

"Legs too skinny?"

"Unlez yoo're trying to zell toozpickz," Mr. Musclez said.

Fortunately for all of us, Photo Guy took our word, and I didn't have to bare my bony knees.

Unfortunately for all of us, he had another idea. "Fritz!" he called to his assistant. "The body suit!"

"Ze vhat?" Mr. Musclez asked.

"We save it only for dire emergencies." Glancing at me, he added, "And believe me, we're definitely talking dire."

A moment later Fritz appeared, handed me a plastic, flesh-colored shirt, and told me to put it on. After warning everyone to look away, I took my shirt off and slipped his on. Next, Franz attached a bicycle pump hose to an opening in the sleeve, and before I knew it

voosh-aa, voosh-aa, voosh-aa

he was literally "pumping me up."

No kidding. It was amazing. I watched as the air pockets in the sleeves and chest began filling up, making it look like I had major muscles.

Franz paused to catch his breath. "How much more, Boss?" he asked.

Photo Guy gave me a dubious look. "In his case, give it all you got. Fill 'er to the limit."

The assistant nodded and resumed. Bigger and bigger my arms grew, thicker and thicker my chest became. It was incredible.

"Good show." Photo Guy nodded. "Good show. And now for a little makeup, to blend in the edges." He gave his fingers a snap, and Fritz was smearing flesh-colored makeup all around the shirt's cuffs, collar, and waistband, carefully blending them into my own skin.

"Wow," I said, checking myself out in a nearby mirror. "I look awesome."

"You got that right, mate," Photo Guy said proudly.

I stepped closer to the mirror, doing various World Wide Wrestling poses with, of course, the appropriate sound effects:

Errr . . . !
Argh . . . !
Grrr . . . !

"Just let Bruno or any of the boys try to give me a swirlee now," I said, stepping right up to the mirror and growling at myself.

"Right," Photo Guy said. "But keep in mind it's only make-believe, mate. And be careful. It's already inflated to the max, so don't be puncturing it."

"Puncturing it?" I asked, turning to him. "How could I possibly—" That was about as far as I got before my elbow, which was a lot bigger than it used to be, smashed into the mirror. As the glass shattered, it fell onto the floor in a million sharp, jagged pieces. Well, actually, 999,999 sharp, jagged pieces. It seems one piece decided to jam itself into my overinflated body suit.

Well, now I knew what he meant by "puncturing it."

Actually, it wasn't that big of a deal, except for the part where all of the air

PSSSSSSSSSSS . . .

rushed out of that one little hole, which managed to jet-propel me

"Auuuuuuuuuuuuuuuuuuuuuuuuuuuuuuuuuuuuuuuuuuuuuu
nnnnnnnnnnnnnnnnnnnnnnnnnnnnnnn
nnnnnnnnnnnnnnn
uuuuuuuuuuuuuuuuuuuuuuuuuuuuuuuuuuuuuuu
nnnnnnnnnnnnnnnnnnnnnnnnnnnnnn
nnnnnnnnnnnnnnnnnnnnnnnnn
uuuuuuuuuuuuuuuuuuuuuuuuuugggghhhh . . ."

all over the room, like an out-of-control rocket that's had way too much caffeine.

Not a major problem—well, except for the part where

"LOOK OUT!"
K-rash, K-slam, K-bamb

I knocked over all the lights on all the light stands. Then, of course, there was the little collision with the huge photo backdrop:

K-smack
teeter-back, teeter-forth, teeter-back, teeter—
"TIMBER!"
K-BOOOM

There was, however, one major problem:
"Oh, no, mate, not me camera, it cost fifty-thousand—

K-there goes my college savings

dollars."
After wiping out everything we could find in the studio, and then some, Air Shirt and I finally ran out of fuel and made a perfect, three-point landing on . . .

K-bump (my rear),
K-thud (my head),
K-squash (my face).

Now, at last, I was safe. Well, except for the shouting and hysterical screaming by Photo Guy: "Get outta me studio! Get outta me studio!"

And his wild swinging at us with anything he could get his hands on—broken light stands, broken cameras, broken assistants.

"I zink ve better go!" Mr. Musclez shouted as he scooped me off the floor and raced for the door. "Not to vorry, Vally. I haf vone more plan. It iz a bit extreme, but it iz all ve haf levt."

"Mondermull," I groaned. "Musst Mondermull." Which, if my jaw had not been broken in fifteen places (that third part of the three-point landing really did me in), would have sounded a lot like:

"Wonderful . . . just wonderful."

Chapter 6

At Any Cost?

"Where are we going now?" Wall Street asked as we turned into a dark, narrow alley.

"To vizit my good vriend, Junior Vizkid."

"Who?"

"He iz a yoong infenter. Iv ve can't get yoor body in zhape, zen ve vill vix ze zkateboard an make it go fazter."

"Fix the skateboard?" I asked. "Isn't that illegal?"

Wall Street and Mr. Musclez exchanged glances.

"Guys," I repeated, "if we fix up the skateboard with a bunch of inventions, isn't that like cheating?"

No one gave an answer as we turned and started down some steep concrete steps.

"Guys?" I asked. "Yo, guys?"

Finally, Wall Street turned to me. "Look, Wally. You want to win, don't you?"

"Well, yeah, but—"

"And what do I always say about winning?"

"Invest in stocks when they're low and sell when—"

"No, no, besides that," she said.

"Uh . . ."

"Stay focused, and don't let anyone or anything get in your way."

"Yeah, but—"

"After all the pain you've been through, don't you want to give it everything you've got?"

"Yeah, but—"

"And, if this is what it takes to win, then this is what we'll do to win."

I had a real good argument in mind. Something that began with "yeah" and ended in "but." Unfortunately, we were interrupted by Mr. Musclez's banging on the steel door at the bottom of the steps.

"Who is present?" a tiny voice squeaked from the other side.

"It'z uz," Mr. Musclez answered.

There were a bunch of clicks, clacks, and rattles as about a hundred locks were unlocked. Then, ever so slowly, the door . . .

creakkk-ed

opened to reveal a dark, deserted tunnel.

Wall Street and I traded nervous looks.

"Couldn't we meet him someplace less creepy?" I asked.

"Like vhere?" Mr. Musclez asked.

"Oh, I don't know—a funeral home, a cemetery, maybe a nice burial crypt?"

Wall Street gave a nervous swallow, then repeated, as much for herself as for me, "Don't let anything or anyone get in your way . . ." With a deep breath, she started forward.

After a few deep breaths of my own (along with plenty of whimpering, oh, and prayers, prayers are very important in this type of situation), I followed. Gradually, as my eyes got used to the dark, I had to admit it wasn't as scary as I thought. Well, except for the cobwebs, the hanging bats, and a giant spider racing toward us.

"GIANT SPIDER RACING TOWARD US?!" (Sorry, didn't mean to scream.)

"A giant spider racing toward us?!" (Is this better?)

Anyway, the critter was about two feet high, four feet around, and scampering toward us with a definite look of *"Oh boy, lunch!"* in its eyes.

"OH BOY, LUNCH! IN ITS EYES!" (Sorry.)

Now it was time for each of us to go into action. For each of us to do what we do best. For . . .

—Wall Street to whip out a credit card and try to buy her way out.

—For me to faint.

—And for Mr. Musclez to reach out with his bare hands and kinda

K-rash,
rattle, rattle, rattle

smash the critter to smithereens.

Wait a minute! Bugs don't go *K-rash, rattle, rattle, rattle* when you hit them. They go *K-squish*. The only things that go *K-rash, rattle, rattle, rattle* are—

"My mechanical spider," the little voice cried. "Observe what you have inflicted upon my mechanical spider!" Suddenly, a little guy (he must have been all of seven) with a little remote control in his little hands appeared.

"Now, Junior," Mr. Musclez said. "I'f told yoo vonze, I'f told yoo a zousand timez. Yoo muzt not zcare and torture yoor gueztz."

"I do apologize," the little guy said as he kicked at the floor. "However, it was one of my more favored." (The kid may look seven, but he sounded like he was seventy.)

"Yoo can alwaze make anozer vone," Mr. Musclez said. "Now, did yoo get my mezzage?"

The kid's eyes brightened. "Certainly. I have constructed several of the articles you mentioned from which you may select. Follow me."

With that, the boy genius turned and headed down the tunnel toward another room.

Once again, Wall Street and I exchanged glances. And, having not learned our lesson the first time around, we, of course, followed.

* * * * *

Junior arrived at the end of the tunnel and opened another door. He hit a switch, and the lights flickered on to reveal this incredible workshop. I mean the place had more blinking lights and sci-fi stuff than an old sci-fi movie rerun. And there, in the center of the room, was a long workbench with about a dozen skateboards on it.

"Wow!" Wall Street said as we headed toward the bench. "Check them out!"

The tops of the boards looked average enough. They were all bright red and had the same Sizzlin' Skateboards logo on them. But underneath, well, underneath they were anything but average. Each of them had all sorts of boxes and gyros and gizmos attached to them.

"I zee yoo'f been buzy," Mr. Musclez said.

"Apparently so," Junior replied, pushing up his glasses.

"Vell, zhow uz vhat yoo'f got."

Junior Whiz Kid began his game of show and tell. He took the closest board off the workbench and set it on the floor. "Here we go." He nodded to Wall Street. "Please, proceed to step upon it."

"Uh, actually"—I cleared my throat—"I'm the one doing the racing."

Junior looked at me, sized up my incredible anti-athleticness, then nearly busted a gut laughing.

"No, seriously," I said.

Junior kept right on laughing.

"I em avraid he'z right, Junior," Mr. Musclez said. "He iz ze vone ve muzt help vin ze raze."

Suddenly, Junior stopped laughing. He looked to me, then to Musclez, then back to me. "Certainly, you are not serious?" he asked. (It's nice to get respect from even the youngest crowd.)

In answer to his question, we all nodded our heads.

The kid's cheery smile turned to a serious frown. "Well, then," he said as he motioned to the workbench, "these are most inappropriate for your needs. They are designed to break only a few rules. What you need are the more elaborate cheating machines. Please, follow me."

I threw a concerned look to Wall Street and mouthed the words, *Cheating machines?*

She nodded and quietly quoted, *"'Don't let anything or anyone get in your way.'"*

Before I could answer, Junior arrived at a smaller table and was setting another skateboard on the floor.

"What does that one do?" I asked as we approached.

"It polarizes your molecular makeup, aligning itself with specific light waves so that—"

"Englizh, Junior," Mr. Musclez interrupted. "Englizh."

"Oh, certainly," he answered, pushing up his glasses. "Basically, it makes you invisible. When you step onto it you become—"

"Pass!" I quickly interrupted.

"You do not wish to test it?"

I shook my head.

"It's a long story," Wall Street explained.

"Actually, it's a whole book," I said. *"My Life As Invisible Intestines."*

"My life az vhat?" Mr. Musclez asked.

"Never mind. What else do you have?"

With a heavy sigh, Junior reached for another board and set it on the ground. "This is a bit more dangerous. I have christened it 'The Think-o-matic.'"

"What's it do?" I asked.

"It transforms your brain waves into action."

"What?"

"Step upon it and observe."

I hesitated.

"'Don't let anything or anyone . . . ,'" Wall Street quoted.

I turned to her. "Even my being a coward?"

She gave a nod. "Even your being a coward. Just think safe thoughts."

"Yeah, right," I sighed. So, with that helpful suggestion (and thoughts of hiding under the covers of my bed), I stepped onto the skateboard, when suddenly:

K-WOOSHHH . . .

Everything blurred, then went black.

"AUGH!" I cried. "What happened? Where am I? What's going on?"

"What were you thinking?" Junior asked.

I heard his voice but couldn't see him. "Where are you?" I shouted.

"I am conversing with you through a speaker on the skateboard. Now tell me, what were you thinking when you stepped upon the board?"

"I don't know . . . just how I wish I was back at home hiding under the covers of my bed."

"Then, reach up to your head and proceed to remove the covers."

"What?"

"Remove the covers."

"That's crazy!"

"Do vhat he zayz, Vally."

I reached to the top of my head and . . . sure enough, I felt blankets. I quickly pulled them aside, and, sure enough again, there I was in my own bed in my own bedroom.

"Wow!" I cried. "How'd you do that?"

"I didn't," Junior's voice said. "You did. You were transported to where you thought."

"No kidding?! So, all I have to do is think of someplace and I'm there?"

"Precisely."

"Cool." I crawled out of my bed, set down the skateboard, and hopped on it again. That's when I saw two or three of Opera's Chippy Chipper potato chip bags lying on the floor from last night. *Man*, I thought, *this guy leaves a mess wherever he goes. I can just guess what his own room looks—*

K-WOOSHHH . . .

Everything blurred, and suddenly I was in another room. Another room with a ton more potato chip bags and one very frightened

"AUGH!"

friend.

"Hey, Opera," I said, trying to sound casual. "How's it going?"

"Wally?" he cried, looking up from his Alien Pig Invaders video game. "Is that you?!" His surprise might have had something to do with him sitting around in his underwear (not a pretty sight). Though I suspect it had more to do with me not knocking before I came in . . . (or not even opening the door). "How'd you do that?" he cried. "Where'd you come from?!"

"Wally, what is your location?" Junior's voice called from the skateboard.

"Who . . . who said that?" Opera stuttered. "What's going on?"

"It's nothing to worry about," I said, grinning.

He looked majorly skeptical.

I skated the board closer to his bed.

"NO!" he cried. "Stay away!"

"Opera . . ."

"I don't know what planet you're from or why you've taken over Wally's body, but—"

"Opera . . ."

"Stay away! Please! Please, don't vaporize me!" (The guy definitely needed to cut back on his video games.)

"Opera . . ."

He scooped up his nearest bag of Chippy Chippers and cowered against the wall. (I guess if he was going, he was going with his chips.) "Stay back! Stay back!!"

Poor guy. He was definitely scared in a *Halloween XXXVI* kind of way.

"Oper—"

"Stay back!!"

As he shouted, I caught a glimpse inside his mouth, all crammed with prechewed potato chips. *Man*, I thought, *how gross is that*, when suddenly

K-WOOSHHH . . .

Another blur. Only this time I felt myself shrinking as I was moving. Shrinking and moving into . . . now it was my turn to scream,

"AUGH!"

because now, I was inside Opera's mouth!

"Augh!" he screamed.

"Augh!!" I screamed.

"Augh!!!" he screamed even louder.

"Vally, vhere are yoo now?" Mr. Musclez's voice shouted.

"Augh!!!!"

"Augh!!!!"

Now, as much as I liked playing "dueling screams," I figured I had other things to do. Like get out of there before he decided to swallow! So, as quickly as possible, I imagined myself back in Junior's lab, and

K-WOOSHHH . . .

there I was. Just me, the skateboard, and about a ton of Chippy Chipper prechewed goo all over my clothing.

"Eewww . . ." Wall Street cringed. "Where were you?"

"It's a long story," I groaned, scraping off some of the goo. I stepped from the board, turned to Junior, and said, "You don't have anything else, do you?"

He looked at me and slowly nodded.

Unfortunately, he had one more. . . .

Chapter 7
Another Snub

Without a word, Junior Genius reached up to the table and grabbed the last and final skateboard. It looked just like the others . . . well, except for the two silver rockets strapped onto each side.

"What is it?" Wall Street asked.

"You are beholding my greatest invention to date. The world's one and only . . . rocket-powered skateboard."

"Cool," Wall Street said.

Junior flipped up a hidden lid on top of the board and switched some switches, dialed some dials, and knobbed some knobs. Immediately, Ol' Superboard began to hum.

"Way cool," Wall Street repeated as she took a couple of steps backward. Of course, if it was so cool, I wondered why she was stepping backward, instead of forward. Must be girl's intuition . . . either that, or memories of all my other misadventures.

"How does it work?" I asked.

"It is self-propelled by these two jets you see on either side," Junior said.

"What are these three little buttons on top?" I asked.

"Those are your speed controls. This green is for traveling up to fifty miles per hour. And this blue is for traveling up to one hundred miles per hour."

I nodded. "And this last button?" I asked. "This red one?" I started to reach for it, but he immediately grabbed my hand.

"That," he said, "is the only button you must *not* use."

"Why, 'cause it goes *over* one hundred miles per hour?" I asked.

"That and more."

"No kidding."

"Actually, we are currently unaware of its limitations. We are still experimenting with it, which is why it is the one button you *must never* touch."

I nodded slowly and understood.

"Would you care to step onto it?" Junior asked.

I gave Mr. Musclez a look, and he nodded. I

turned to Wall Street and she nodded, too, before taking another step backward. (Good ol' Wall Street.)

Actually, I figured I couldn't do that much damage just by stepping onto the board. And I would have been right, too, except (and there's always an "except" in these situations) I accidentally stepped on my shoelace when I was stepping onto the board. Even that wouldn't have been so bad, if I hadn't performed my world-famous B. R. McDoogle trip—("B. R." as in: "**B**one **R**earranging"; "McDoogle" as in: "**You know it's going to hurt**"). Actually, it's a complex move, patented worldwide, that has taken me several books to perfect. Fortunately, it landed me on the board safely enough. Unfortunately, it also landed me on the little green button . . .

The little green button that sent Superboard shooting off at fifty miles per hour.

The good news was, I immediately fell off and didn't break a single body part.

The bad news was, after

*K-zing*ing

off one wall and

*K-ping*ing

off another, Ol' Superboard got kind of frisky and

*K-rash*ed
*tinkle, tinkle, tinkle*d

through the one and only window.

"Sorry," I said, giving a feeble shrug.

Junior just looked at the hole and shook his head in amazement.

"Everyone's good at something," I explained. "For me, it's disasters."

"Ve are zorry, Junior," Mr. Musclez said.

Junior nodded.

"Pity. It vaz our vavorite board, too."

"Well, then," Junior said with a heavy sigh, "you are quite fortunate."

"Why are we fortunate?" I asked.

"We are working on a similar model and should have it ready for you by the race Saturday."

I smiled weakly. (This was obviously a new definition of "fortunate.")

"Terrivic," Mr. Musclez exclaimed. "Zat'z juzt terrivic."

My smile grew weaker. (This was obviously a new definition of "terrivic.")

"So we're all ready." Wall Street beamed. "We have the skateboard, we have the team behind the skateboard, and—"

"We just need the rider who can stay on the skateboard," I mumbled.

"Not to vorry," Mr. Musclez said, slapping me on the back (and dislocating a vertebra or two). "A vew more dayz ov vorking out, and yoo'll be ready."

Actually, I figured a few more "dayz ov vorking out" and I'd be in the hospital, but I didn't want to disappoint the guy (or miss out on any of the fun and pain). So, I simply nodded and turned to head back for the gym. Ah, the gym, the place where I'd be living for the rest of the week. My home away from home, where I'd work out and work out and then take a break by working out some more. Yes sir, the gym. Groan sweet groan . . .

* * * * *

Three days had passed. Junior worked on his skateboard, Mr. Musclez worked on me, and I worked on surviving.

And Wall Street? She stayed right at my side. "Focus, focus, focus. . . . Don't let anything or anyone get in your way." That had become like our motto.

Of course, there were other people working in the gym with other mottos:

"Let's go, Brunnie. GO! GO! GO!"

That's right, Bruno and his dad were still there.

"We've gotta beat this jerk, son. Come on! Let's GO, GO, GO!"

Poor kid. Even when we were running on the treadmills together (well, he was running, I was busy wheezing out a lung or two), I usually felt sorry for him.

"Hey, McLoser," he shouted, "come Saturday, you're gonna be dead meat!!"

(Usually.)

By the time Friday night rolled around, I was feeling closer to being in shape than ever. Well, "in shape" might not be the right phrase, but at least there were fewer broken body parts and fewer organs to transplant than on Monday. So, now I lay in bed, trying to get some sleep for the big race tomorrow.

Of course, Opera and little Leroy had phoned me a couple of dozen times throughout the week. After all, I'd promised to help them build that model car. And tomorrow was also the day of that model car derby. But I couldn't be bothered with such trivia. I mean, we're talking the Cross-Country Skateboard Championship of the Universe, right? It was a hundred times more important than some kid with some stupid model car race.

"Focus, focus, focus. . . . Don't let anything or anyone get in your way."

At least that's what I kept telling myself. But for some reason I couldn't shake little Leroy and my promises. So, I did what anyone would do. Well, anyone with a laptop computer and a guilty conscience. I popped open Ol' Betsy to work on my Kid Giver and Greedy Guy story. I was at the part where he's looking for his brother's hideout. . . .

`In desperately deep desperation, our heroic hero heroically hunts, hollers, hails, and—`

`"Look, can we just get on with the story?!"` a voice interrupts.

`I glance around my room, then nervously type:` Who, who said that?

`"It's me, the bad guy!"`

`I type:` But I'm the author.

`"So?"`

So, you can't interrupt the writer.

`"I can when he goes on and on with all that stupid alliteration."`

Alliter—what?

`"It's when you start a bunch of words with the same letter."`

So there's a name for that?

"Of course there is." He sighs. "I
thought you were an author."

I am, but it didn't dawn on my dynamically
dense dimwittedness that—

"Look, just tell my brother I'm
waiting for him at our old house."

Why don't you?

"Because that would mean **GIVING**
him information, and I don't **GIVE** anything, remember?"

Oh, yeah.

"I tell you, for a bad guy, I have
to do everything around here."

Sorry, I type. Thanks for being so for-
GIVING and for—

"Stop it."

—**GIVING** me a hand.

"I said, knock it off."

I had some misgivings, but you really are—

"Stop!"

—giving me hope.

"All right! All right! I'll tell
him, I'll tell him! Just knock off
the stupid **GIVING** jokes. They're as
bad as your alliteration!"

Before I can type an answer, let alone leave
a lengthy list of letters listing line by line the
location leading to his lair—

"Kid Giver! Kid Giver, I'm at the old house!" Greedy Guy shouts. "If you can hear me, hurry and meet me at the old house, before he writes any more!"

"I hear you," Kid Giver shouts from somewhere in the back of my imagination. "I'm on my way!"

I stared at the screen a moment, unable to go on. I don't know what it was, but somehow I was feeling a lot like Greedy Guy, at least when it came to Opera and Leroy.

But it was time to get some rest. I shut Ol' Betsy down, turned off the light, and closed my eyes. Tomorrow was going to be a busy day. If I won, it would radically change my life. Not only would I have all of that worldly fame (not to mention worldly money), but I'd have to resign as president of Dorkoids Anonymous. (It's hard to be a dorkoid when you're a superstar.)

Terrible sacrifices, I know. But they were sacrifices I'd be willing to make. After all, I had worked hard, and I had *focused, focused, focused . . . not letting anything or anyone get in my way.*

Chapter 8

Let the Race Begin . . .

It was a zoo with three hundred fifty of us at the starting line. We were the top three winners from the preliminary races held around the world last week. As you may remember, the winners from my race were:

1. **Bonnie the Brain**, who was now frantically hooking up solar panels to her arms and legs—"Thereby utilizing photoelectric power to its optimum potential," she explained.

2. **Bruno the Bruiser**—"Hope you know a good undertaker," he sneered.

3. **And me**— "Or a hospital," I muttered.

Actually, there was one other racer from our group. A person who looked a lot like Slacker

Sam (well, except for the extra head and seven arms that seemed to be made of cotton stuffing). I don't want to say the guy was cheating, but since he hadn't qualified in our race last week, he claimed he had qualified in his hometown race on the planet Jupiter.

Of course, there was the usual worldwide panic that we were being invaded by aliens, and the calling out of the National Guard. But, in the spirit of intergalactic goodwill (and fear that they would be de-molecularized by his neutron beam), the race officials finally agreed to let him participate.

So, there they were, three hundred forty-nine of the top racers in the world (er, universe) . . . and me.

It was a long course the officials had laid out through our town. And what made it even more interesting was that it was divided into different sections, each section representing some part of the world.

"SKATERS, ON YOUR MARK!" the official shouted.

Mr. Musclez set the new and improved Superboard on the pavement. "Juzt remember," he said. "Green iz vor trafeling up to vivty milez per hour, blue iz vor vone hundred milez per hour, and red iz—"

"For not touching," I interrupted.

"Prezizely."

"And we'll be monitoring the whole race through a camera on your helmet," Wall Street said. "If you get in a jam, we'll give you instructions through your headset."

I nodded.

"GET SET!" the official shouted.

I stepped on the board. My heart was pounding harder than speakers inside a rapper's car.

"Focus, focus, focus," Wall Street whispered.

"Don't die, don't die, don't die," I nervously agreed.

And then it happened. Some madman in the crowd started firing a gun.

"Augh!" I cried, leaping from the skateboard and trying to hide under it. "Get down, get down!"

"Wally!" Wall Street shouted.

"Someone's got a gun!" I yelled, trying to pull her to safety. "Get down, get—"

"Wally, that's the starting pistol!"

"What?"

"The official's starting pistol!"

With incredible courage (just slightly greater than my incredible ignorance), I raised my head to take a look.

"Hurry!" she shouted. "The race has started! The race has started!"

Now, I'm not saying she was right, but there was something about the way all three hundred forty-nine of the other racers took off, leaving me in the dust, that seemed kinda convincing. That and Mr. Musclez screaming: "Hurry, Vally! Hurry! Hurry!"

The time had come. It was now or never. And, though I preferred "never," I hopped onto Ol' Superboard and shoved off. We had a long way to go, and I figured there was no time like the present to begin the pain and suffering.

First up was the same steep city street (say that seven times fast) that we had raced on last week. Everyone used it to build up their speed. Well, everyone else used it to build up their speed. But, since we already know of my unique habit for getting into the wrong lane at the wrong time, I'll save you all the gory My-Life-As-a-Semi-Truck-Hood-Ornament details and just say it wasn't a pretty sight.

Once the paramedics reset all the bones in my body (did you know there are two hundred six of them—see how educational these books can be?) and restarted my heart, I hopped back onto the board and raced toward the next location . . . the city zoo.

I don't want to say I was running late, but by the time I got there I noticed they'd already surveyed, built, and opened up an entirely new freeway between me and the zoo (either that or I was majorly lost). In any case, I zipped across the multiple lanes with only a couple of close

HONK-HONK
SQUEAL-SQUEAL
K-RASH, K-RASH

calls until, at last, I made it into the zoo itself.

The officials tried to make this part of the race like Africa, which was pretty cool. It might have been cooler without the man-eating (or is it dork-eating?) lions that became part of my mini-safari.

Still, you really can't blame the officials. I mean, how'd they know some out-of-control racer would

"LOOK OUT! COMING THROUGH!"

head down the main walkway at just under the speed of light until he

K-Thunk!

hit the statue of our beloved mayor, Morton K. Finklestink, and went flying straight toward the caged lions?

The good news was, the bars of the cage were close enough to keep the skateboard

K-clink

outside. The bad news was, they let the

"AUGH!!!"

skinny skateboarder inside.

So, there I was having a little face-to-fang meeting with Leo Boy, which was okay until he started doing his MGM roaring lion imitation, which caused me to start doing my McDoogle screaming coward routine.

Even that wasn't so bad, until he made it clear that he wanted me to stay for a bite to eat, which was thoughtful until I realized that *I* was the bite. So, after carefully rising to my feet and edging toward the edge of the cage, . . .

"Nice, kitty-kitty . . ."
"ROAR!!!"

I dove back through the bars and crashed onto the sidewalk.

I leaped back onto my board and took off toward the South American part of the race.

The part that involved going past the crocodile exhibit. Actually, it wasn't the "going past" that bothered me as much as my accidentally "going through." "Going through," as in:

SNAP! SNAP!
"Yikes! Yikes!"
SNAP! SNAP! SNAP!
"Yikes! Yikes! Yikes!"
SNAP! SNAP! SNAP! SNAP!
"Yikes! Yikes! Yi—" (Well, you get the idea.)

Don't get me wrong, it's not that I'm prejudiced against reptiles or anything (though I prefer the type that eats flies instead of people). But, figuring I'd already been crocodile junk food once in my life, I decided to look for another way to inflict permanent bodily harm.

So, as much as I hated cheating, but unable to break my habit of wanting to live, I reluctantly reached down to Ol' Superboard, took a deep breath, and pressed the green button.

K-swoosh!

Next stop, the city's garbage dump.

Chapter 9

K-VOOM!

Now I suppose the first question you have is, why a cross-country skateboard race through a garbage dump? The answer is simple . . .

I don't know. (But if anyone has a clue, e-mail me.)

Actually, I suppose since the officials wanted us to pretend to be traveling through the world, it probably had something to do with us appreciating how awful the starving, Third World slums are. Of course, instead of going through a garbage dump, we could just as well have gone through Burt's (or is it Brock's?) bedroom, but I guess they had to make sure we got out alive.

Luckily, at fifty miles an hour, the garbage dump would be a fast trip. Already I was catching up and passing the slowest of the racers . . .

"Look out!"
swish, swish

"Coming through!"
swish, swish, swish

like there was no tomorrow (which, in my case, could very well be true).

Finally, in front of me, I saw Slacker Sam. He would have been farther ahead except for the extra hitchhikers hanging on to his fake head and arms. Hitchhikers who looked an awful lot like junkyard dogs. Junkyard dogs that just happened to like champing into cotton-stuffed heads and arms and shaking them back and forth in their mouths.

"Help me!" Sammy Boy shouted as I zoomed past.

For the briefest second I thought of slowing down and giving him a hand, until I heard Wall Street's voice crackle through my headset. "Don't let anything or anyone get in your way."

"Sorry!" I shouted as I roared by. And I was. But Wall Street was right. I couldn't slow down for that.

Traveling at this speed definitely had its advantages. There was, however, one little problem I found, and it involved my steering.

I couldn't!!!

Which would explain all of my

*K-lang*ing, *K-bang*ing, *K-whamm*ing

through the piles of broken-down clothes washers, clothes dryers, and the ever-popular broken-down sofas. Broken-down sofas that had more than their fair share of springs. Springs that, when hit just right (or in my case, just wrong), could

K-boing

send you flying high into the air, which is also kinda cool until you realize you're heading right into the giant car crusher.

"THE GIANT CAR CRUSHER?!"

(I'm yelling again, aren't I? Sorry.)

You know, those giant machines that smash old wrecks into something flat enough for The House of Pancakes? No problem, except I'm a *young* wreck, and I hate pancakes, especially if I'm mistaken for one.

But there I was, heading straight toward the *early bird breakfast menu* as the giant crusher came straight down at me.

"HIT ZE BLUE BUTTON!" Mr. Musclez's voice shouted over my headset.

I didn't have to be told twice. I kicked the blue button with my foot and

K-VOOM!

sped up to one hundred miles per hour, leaving the car crusher behind.

"WOO-WEE!" I shouted, traveling so fast that my cheeks were flapping somewhere back around my ears.

Up ahead I spotted the next portion of my personal torture . . . river rafting. The good news was, the officials didn't need to make up a fake river; my town had a real one.

The bad news was, well . . . my town had a real one.

So, as the other racers were busy building their little rafts to get across the water, I just kept on

*V-ROOM*ing,

which allowed me to go

*skip skip skip*ping

across the water like a stone on a lake. Not bad, except for the minor problem of that houseboat directly in my path . . .

"Look out! Coming thro—"
K-rippp . . .

which suddenly gave new meaning to the terms "split-level" and "sunken living room."

Then there was that rather unfortunate incident with the fisherman and his rowboat. But, at least he was wearing a

"AUGH!"
K-splinter-to-smithereens

life jacket.

Up ahead, I spotted Bonnie the Brain decked out in all her solar panels. But instead of moving, she floated motionless on the water.

"What's wrong?" I shouted.

"The sun!" she yelled, pointing to the sky.

I looked up. "What sun? All I see are clouds."

"Exactly!" she cried. "Without the sun, these solar panels are useless."

Poor kid. Giant tears were already streaming down her cheeks. I leaned slightly to the left and started circling her. That's when I noticed the giant waterfall. The giant waterfall that she was floating straight toward.

"Here!" I shouted, moving in closer. "Grab my arm. I'll pull you to shore."

She looked up at me, her face beaming.

"Wally!" Wall Street's voice blasted through my headset. "What are you doing?!"

"She's in trouble!" I shouted. "She needs my—"

"Don't let anything or anyone—"

"I know, but she's going over those falls!"

"She's your opponent, Wally. If you help her now, she might come back and beat you later!"

"Yeah, but—"

"Anything or anyone!"

I looked at Bonnie. She smiled and reached out her hand to me.

"Anything or anyone, Wally!" Wall Street yelled.

There was no missing the hope in Bonnie's eyes.

"You've worked too hard to blow it now!"

Our hands were just a few inches apart.

"Anything or anyone!"

We were nearly touching.

"Anything or anyone!"

And then, at the last second, I pulled my hand back and zoomed past her.

She let out a little scream of surprise as I raced by, but I didn't look back. I felt too dirty. Too creepy. Too guilty. Besides, that little scream of surprise would be nothing compared to the big scream she'd be letting loose when she went over the falls. They weren't high enough to hurt her, but definitely high enough to put her out of the race.

"All right, Vally! Zat a boy!" Mr. Musclez shouted.

"Way to go, Wally!"

But the cheering over my headset did little to relieve the guilt. Actually, it was more than guilt. It was realizing that I was becoming something I'd never been before. Something I never wanted to be . . .

A jerk.

"Focus, Wally, focus," Wall Street's voice crackled. "You're almost home. Put her out of your mind and focus!"

I nodded and tried to obey. The riverbank was just ahead. And beyond that . . . beyond that was my ol' pal Bruno the Bruiser. He was at the head of the pack, skating for all he was worth toward our city's one and only skyscraper. So far in the race, we'd covered most of the landforms . . . well, except for mountains. And, since there was a grand total of zero mountains in our town (other than Mrs. Snivelips's front-yard collection of molehills), the skyscraper would have to do.

Bruno had just entered the building and was starting up the stairs (no small feat on a skateboard, but, like I said, he was good). I zoomed up behind him and tried to pass on the left. He spotted me over his shoulder and . . .

K-thud
"Ow!"

cut me off. Next, I tried to pass on the right and

K-thud
"Ow!"

I met a repeat in the blockage department.

So, on and on we went, one floor after another. Every time I tried to get by, he would cut me off. Did I say he was good? He was better than good. He was incredible! I mean, here I was cruising on rocket power, and he was sweating and gasping and panting on his own power—and *still* he was able to beat me! The guy was amazing, doing it all on his own.

Well, almost on his own. He did have a little help from Mr. Bruiser's yelling. Did I say a little? Actually, his dad was shouting so loud through his headset that I could hear him screaming from half a flight of stairs behind.

"Let's go, boy. Go! Go! Go!"

"I'm trying, Dad," Bruno gasped.

"Trying's not good enough! Nobody remembers tryers, only winners!"

"But (pant, gasp), Dad . . ."

"Go! Go! Go!"

"Dad (gasp, pant) . . ."

"No excuses! Win! Win! Win!"

Once again I felt bad about the way Mr. Bruiser kept pushing his son. I mean, it seemed like winning was the only thing he cared about, like it was the only reason he loved his kid.

"Go! Go! Go! Win! Win! Win!"

Maybe it was. Which would explain why, once we reached the top of the stairs and started going down them, he suddenly shouted new instructions.

"Open the doors to the floors as you pass them! Open the doors into McDorkle's face so he smashes into them!"

"But, Dad—"

"You heard me, boy!"

"That's cheating."

"Of course it is!"

"But—"

"It's not how you win the game that counts, it's *if* you win. Go! Go! Go! Win! Win! Win!"

And so, with his dad's encouragement, Bruno started opening each floor's door as he passed them, which means I

*K-smash, K-smash, K-smash*ed

into each floor's door as I went through them. Not a real problem, except the building was eighty-nine stories, which meant eighty-nine openings and eighty-nine

*K-smash*ings.

To say I was a little woozy was like saying, "Water is a little wet."

Actually, more like saying, "Broken faces can sometimes be a pain."

No, more like saying, "Multiple concussions aren't your friend."

No, more like . . . well, you get the picture. The point is, by the time we got to the bottom floor, I was so punch-drunk, I should have called a designated skater. But I didn't, so there I was, doing little figure eights around and around inside the lobby singing my favorite delirious ditty:

"la-la-la-la-la-la . . ."

as Bruiser Boy shot out the door and headed for the finish line over at Skateboard Park.

"He's getting away!" Wall Street shouted over my headset.

"Hurry, Vally!" Mr. Musclez screamed. "He'z going to vin!"

"That's nice." I smiled as I continued my

*"la-la-la-la-la-la*ing . . ."
(Okay, so the words aren't great, but
they're the best my unconscious mind
could come up with on such short notice.)

"Now, Wally!" Wall Street yelled. "Get back outside and fire up your Superboard, now!"

"All—*la-la-la-la-la*—right . . ."

I mumbled as I turned toward the exit and

Bamb! "Ouch"
Bamb! "Ouch"
Bamb! "Ouch"

hit every wall I could find till I finally found the glass door, which was okay except for the part about

Bamb!—shatter, shatter, shatter

forgetting to open it before I went through.

But that didn't stop Wall Street and Mr. Musclez from continuing to shout:

"He's almost at the finish line!"

"Hurry, Vally! Yoo're going to looze. Yoo're going to looze!"

So, with that bit of cheery news, I bent down to Ol' Superboard and did the only thing I could do in my half-dazed state. I reached for either the green button or the blue button. But, since my consciousness still wasn't up to speed (as if it ever is), I, of course, hit the . . . you guessed it, red

K-WoooOOOOOOSH!

"AUGHHHHH . . ."

button.

Chapter 10

Wrapping Up

Instantly, my mind cleared. Something about shooting straight up toward the moon at a bazillion miles per hour will do that. Actually, I didn't shoot straight up—I sort of managed a few loop-the-loops in the process and a little screaming. Actually, *a lot* of screaming. It's not that I'm afraid of flying, I'd just prefer to do it inside a plane instead of clinging for my life to a rocket-powered skateboard. Oh, and speaking of planes:

"LOOK OUT!"
SHHHEEEEEEWWWW . . .

The best I could tell, that was either a Boeing 757 or a very high-flying bus with wings (it was hard to notice the details in my condition). However, I did notice several passengers pointing and staring through the window ("Look, Mommy, it's a flying McDoogle.") with someone even taking a flash photo. I did my best to smile (it's always important to look good for your fans), and would have offered to give autographs, but, like I said, I had a few other things on my mind, like, oh, I don't know . . .

SURVIVING! (Sorry, again.)

Eventually, though, I started to get the hang of the flying . . . well, a little. I mean, it only took a couple of birds

tweet-tweet K-POOF!
tweet-tweet K-POOF!

mand ma mouthmull mof meathers—(*K-spit*, sorry)—and a mouthful of feathers before I caught on to steering the thing. Don't get me wrong, it wasn't a great flight—I mean, no one was passing out peanuts or offering to show movies—but the view wasn't bad. Particularly, the view of the race course.

Ah, yes, the race course . . .

Down below were all my favorite hangouts, like the city zoo, the city dump, the city river, the city skyscraper. Such fond memories. Yeah, right. To be honest, they were anything but fond. Because every place I looked reminded me of how I was changing . . . how I was getting creepier.

"Vally, can yoo hear mee?" Mr. Musclez called through my headset. "Vally, are yoo zhere?"

This time, for some reason, I didn't answer.

"Yoo can ztill vin! Juzt turn zat board around. Yoo can crozz ze vinish line bevor him. Yoo can ztill vin!"

I looked down at the finish line. Mr. Musclez was right. Bruno still had about a hundred yards to go. I could spin around and beat him across the finish line, no sweat.

"Wally, can you hear me?!" Wall Street shouted. "Wally?"

I looked off toward the horizon. There was the old Community Church and the parking lot behind it. The very parking lot where Leroy and Opera were no doubt getting ready for the model car derby race. The very race that I'd been promising to help with all week but never did. Poor kid. I still remembered the look on his face when I'd kicked them out of my bedroom. And now today, I'd completely snubbed him.

How had it happened? How had I gone from nice guy to a jerk who only cared about winning?

"Vally, turn around! Turn ze board around!"

Don't get me wrong. There's nothing wrong with winning. But when it becomes all you think about . . .

"Focus, Wally. Focus! Don't think about anything or anyone!"

When it becomes your whole life . . .

I looked back down at the skateboarders. There was Slacker Sam still running for his life. By the look of things, he'd picked up an extra dozen or two stray dogs. Not that he didn't deserve them, but how was his cheating any different from mine? And why hadn't I helped? I mean, cheating or not, those dogs' teeth really hurt.

And there, at the bottom of the waterfall, was Bonnie the Brain swimming toward shore. It didn't look like she was hurt . . . but she could have been. What was wrong with me? Why hadn't I helped?

"Vally, zis iz yoor lazt chanze! Turn ze board around! Yoo can ztill beat him!"

I looked back to the finish line. And Bruno. Winning was so important to him . . . and his dad. It's all they cared about. It's all that mattered to them. It's all they had.

Finally, I turned back to the church parking lot.

"Focus, Wally. Focus, focus, focus!"

So many people affected by me. So many people hurt because of my desire to win at any cost . . .

"Turn around, Vally! Yoo muzt turn around, now!"

Mr. Musclez was right. It *was* time to turn around. But not in the way he was saying. With a deep breath, I leaned hard on the side of the board and veered sharply to the right.

"No, Vally, ze other vay!"

Then I dipped down the nose of the board . . .

"No, Wally! NO!"

. . . and made a beeline straight for the

ZZZZZzzz . . .
"INCOMING . . ."

church parking lot. I didn't know how far they were in the derby, but I knew *that* was the race I should be at. *That* was the place I'd promised to be. *That* was the place I *should* be.

The good news was, I only got tangled up in a couple of telephone wires and only wiped out a couple of

twang . . . *K-thud*
twang . . . *K-thud*

telephone poles. I was also grateful to learn that they were already planning to rebuild that

K-RASH!

church steeple. So, basically, it was a pretty good landing. It was even better when I caught a glimpse of Opera and little Leroy running toward me.

"Wally . . ."

Yes sir, Bruno the Bruiser may be winning the race, but I was winning something else. I don't know exactly how I had changed over the week, but it felt great to be getting back to my old self again (broken bones and all).

Yes sir, it felt great to be doing the right thing, even if I wasn't a winner. Then again, maybe I was more of a winner than I thought.

Of course, it would have felt even greater if I hadn't fallen into unconsciousness (hitting asphalt parking lots can do that to a guy). But even that was okay, because when you're unconscious, sometimes you dream. And the cool thing about dreaming is that sometimes you get to think up endings to superhero stories.

So, with nothing else to do but wait for my paramedic pals to show up and do their usual

lifesaving stuff, I thought back to my story of
Kid Giver and his twin brother, Greedy Gu—

"Hey, why do I always get second
billing?" Greedy Guy demands.

What? I think back.

"How come it's always Kid Giver
and Greedy Guy? What's wrong with me
being named first and my brother
being named last?"

You mean Greedy Guy and Kid Giver?

"Yeah!"

Well, because . . . because . . . (I knew it was
my story and I'd better think of something fast.
And then it came—something I heard back in
Sunday school when I was just a kid.) *"Because
the last shall be first and the first shall be last."*

"What's that mean?"

*I'm not sure, but it might be my subconscious
trying to connect my skateboard race with this
superhero story.*

"What are you talking about?"

Like I said, I'm not sure, but—

"I know, I know!" Kid Giver shouts
as he bursts through the front door
of their old house.

"Oh, brother!" Greedy Guy sighs.

"That's right!" Kid Giver shouts. "I am your brother!" With that he runs over and gives his twin a big hug.

"Augh! Stop it! Stop it with the **GIVING**!"

"But I enjoy **GIVING** hugs. Here, have another!"

"Stop it!" Greedy Guy staggers backward, out of breath. "You came to destroy my Sonic Greed Generator, not **GIVE** me hugs!"

"But I love you." Again he throws his arms around his brother, and again the baddest of bad boys screams in agony:

"AUGH! How can I fight you if all you do is **GIVE** hugs?!"

"Got me. Guess you can't!"

"But where is your sword, or your gun, or at least a good old-fashioned photon laser?"

"Sorry, all I've got is this love."

He throws another hug on Greedy Guy, who shrieks, "I can't take it, I can't take it!"

"But you have to take it, because I'm **GIVING** it."

"NO...NOOO!!" Before he knows it, Greedy Guy's eyes start filling with tears.

"What, pray tell, is the problem?" Kid Giver asks.

After a few *sniff-sniffs*, and one rather loud *SNORT!* (wow, that was impressive), Greedy Guy is finally able to answer. "It's just, all of my life I've tried to be better than you."

"But you are," Kid Giver says, **GIVING** him another compliment. "You beat me at everything we do."

"I may beat you, *sniff,* but I never win."

"What do you mean?"

"I mean, even when I win, you're still the one who is the happiest. Even when you come in in last place, it's like you still wind up in first."

"Ah," Kid Giver says. "Sounds like we're about to **GIVE** the moral of our story."

Greedy Guy nods. "Someone better, *snort,* 'cause we're running out of pages."

"The reason I'm always happy, dear brother, is because there's another type of winning—the winning at life. And sometimes to win that race, you need to lose the other. Sometimes, to really be first, you need to be last."

"Wait a minute, isn't that too deep for a kid's superhero story?"

Kid Giver shrugs. "Maybe, but these readers are smart. Between this story and the skateboard one, they'll figure it out."

"But what's all this got to do with my Sonic Greed Generator?" Greedy Guy asks.

"By making folks take from others," Kid Giver explains, "you actually make them less happy. But if you let them **GIVE**, they'll wind up with more joy."

"Wow!" Greedy Guy cries in excitement. "So people will be happier if I let them start **GIVING**?"

"You've got it."

"No, I want to **GIVE** it."

"What do you mean?"

"I'm going to shut down my Sonic Greed Generator."

"Great."

"And from now on, I'm going to become a superhero known only for my **GIVING**."

"Wait a minute, that's my job. I'm the one who **GIVES** in these stories."

"Not anymore."

"But—"

"What do you think of the name... **GIVER** Guy?"

"But I'm Kid Giver."

"Right, and from now on, **GIVER** Guy is going to out**GIVE** Kid **GIVER**."

"What?!"

"We're going to have battles over who can **GIVE** the most!"

"Uh, I don't think that's the way it's supposed to work."

"It'll be great!"

"You're **GIVING** me a headache."

"See, it's happening already! And about those hugs. You think yours were cool. Check this one out." Suddenly, Greedy Guy—

"That's **GIVER** Guy, if you don't mind."

Sorry. Suddenly, **GIVER** Guy reaches over and **GIVES** his brother a huge bear hug.

"Ow!" Kid **GIVER** cries. Then, catching his breath, he shouts, "Oh yeah, well, here's a bigger one than that!"

"OW!" **GIVER** Guy screams. "Oh yeah! Well, take this."

"*AUGH!* Oh yeah? Take that!"

"*AUGHHH!*"

And so the two brothers once again find another reason to fight as they keep on hugging and trying to outlove and out**GIVE** each other (while completely missing the point to this story).

"Take that!"

"*OW!* Take this!"

"*OW!* Take——"

"Wally . . . *munch, munch,* you awake?"

I slowly opened my eyes to see Opera and little Leroy looking down at me. I was back home in bed. Well, not home, really, more like in the hospital emergency room (sometimes I get those two places mixed up).

"That was some, *crunch, crunch,* landing you made in the parking lot," Opera said.

I gave a small smile (it's hard to give a big

one when your jaw is wired shut). Then I glanced at Leroy. "So how'd you do in the derby?" I mumbled.

"I didn't race," he said.

"Why not?"

Opera answered, "He was too worried about, *burp,* you."

Little Leroy shrugged. "I wanted to visit you here, instead. I know it's stupid, but I was more worried about you than about winning."

My smile grew bigger, and I shook my head. "No, little guy, that's not stupid at all." I wanted to say a lot more. . . . Like that *he* was really the smart one. Like *he* was the one who knew winning isn't everything. But Wall Street suddenly burst into the room.

"Hey, Wally! Too bad about the race," she said.

I nodded.

"Guess you just couldn't control the board, could you?"

I started to answer, but she didn't give me a chance.

"Don't worry," she said. "'Cause you've given me a brand-new idea. I mean, why limit those rockets to just skateboards? I've been talking to Junior Whiz Kid, and he can open up a whole new line of products for us."

I tried to interrupt, but it did no good.

"What do you think of rocket-powered in-line skates?" she asked. "Or rocket-powered tricycles . . . or jump ropes or—and this one is sooo cool— rocket-powered toilet paper?!"

I thought of stopping her, but it would do no good. She was definitely on a roll. And even now, as she kept rattling on, I suspected she'd already dreamed up some new way of using and abusing me.

". . . and you could be like our test pilot . . ."

See what I mean?

". . . because if anything can go wrong, it will go wrong with you . . ."

Isn't it nice to know that as much as some things change, others remain the same?

". . . and since you've got all that medical insurance and since . . ."

I don't know how many more of these little life lessons I'm going to have to learn, but with the help of Wall Street, Opera, Ol' Betsy, and all my pals here in the emergency room, I know one thing. They'll never get boring.

You'll want to read them all.

THE INCREDIBLE WORLDS OF WALLY McDOOGLE

#1—My Life As a Smashed Burrito with Extra Hot Sauce

Twelve-year-old Wally—the "Walking Disaster Area"—is forced to stand up to Camp Wahkah Wahkah's number one all-American bad guy. One hilarious mishap follows another until, fighting together for their very lives, Wally learns the need for even his worst enemy to receive Jesus Christ. (ISBN 0-8499-3402-8)

#2—My Life As Alien Monster Bait

"Hollyweird" comes to Middletown! Wally's a superstar! A movie company has chosen our hero to be eaten by their mechanical "Mutant from Mars"! It's a close race as to which will consume Wally first—the disaster-plagued special effects "monster" or his own out-of-control pride—until he learns the cost of true friendship and of God's command for humility. (ISBN 0-8499-3403-6)

#3—My Life As a Broken Bungee Cord

A hot-air balloon race! What could be more fun? Then again, we're talking about Wally McDoogle, the "Human Catastrophe." Calamity builds on calamity until, with his life on the line, Wally learns what it means to FULLY put his trust in God. (ISBN 0-8499-3404-4)

#4—My Life As Crocodile Junk Food

Wally visits missionary friends in the South American rain forest. Here he stumbles onto a whole new set of impossible predicaments . . . until he understands the need and joy of sharing Jesus Christ with others. (ISBN 0-8499-3405-2)

#5—My Life As Dinosaur Dental Floss

It starts with a practical joke that snowballs into near disaster. Risking his life to protect his country, Wally is pursued by a SWAT team, bungling terrorists, photosnapping tourists, Gary the Gorilla, and a TV news reporter. After prehistoric-size mishaps and a talk with the President, Wally learns that maybe honesty really is the best policy. (ISBN 0-8499-3537-7)

#6—My Life As a Torpedo Test Target

Wally uncovers the mysterious secrets of a sunken submarine. As dreams of fame and glory increase, so do the famous McDoogle mishaps. Besides hostile sea creatures, hostile pirates, and hostile Wally McDoogle clumsiness, there is the war against his own greed and selfishness. It isn't until Wally finds himself on a wild ride atop a misguided torpedo that he realizes the source of true greatness. (ISBN 0-8499-3538-5)

#7—My Life As a Human Hockey Puck

Look out . . . Wally McDoogle turns athlete! Jealousy and envy drive Wally from one hilarious calamity to another until, as the team's mascot, he learns humility while suddenly being thrown in to play goalie for the Middletown Super Chickens! (ISBN 0-8499-3601-2)

#8—My Life As an Afterthought Astronaut

"Just 'cause I didn't follow the rules doesn't make it my fault that the Space Shuttle almost crashed. Well, okay, maybe it was sort of my fault. But not the part when Pilot O'Brien was spacewalking and I accidentally knocked him halfway to Jupiter . . ." So begins another hilarious Wally McDoogle MISadventure as our boy blunder stows aboard the Space Shuttle and learns the importance of: Obeying the Rules! (ISBN 0-8499-3602-0)

#9—My Life As Reindeer Road Kill

Santa on an out-of-control four wheeler? Electrical Rudolph on the rampage? Nothing unusual, just Wally McDoogle doing some last-minute Christmas shopping . . . FOR GOD! Our boy blunder dreams that an angel has invited him to a birthday party for Jesus. Chaos and comedy follow as he turns the town upside down looking for the perfect gift, until he finally bumbles his way into the real reason for the season. (ISBN 0-8499-3866-X)

#10—My Life As a Toasted Time Traveler

Wally travels back from the future to warn himself of an upcoming accident. But before he knows it, there are more Wallys running around than even Wally himself can handle. Catastrophes reach an all-time high as Wally tries to out-think God and rewrite history. (ISBN 0-8499-3867-8)

#11—My Life As Polluted Pond Scum

This laugh-filled Wally disaster includes: a monster lurking in the depths of a mysterious lake . . . a glowing figure with powers to summon the creature to the shore . . . and one Wally McDoogle, who reluctantly stumbles upon the truth. Wally's entire town is in danger. He must race against the clock and his own fears and learn to trust God before he has any chance of saving the day. (ISBN 0-8499-3875-9)

#12—My Life As a Bigfoot Breath Mint

Wally gets his big break to star with his uncle Max in the famous Fantasmo World stunt show. Unlike his father, whom Wally secretly suspects to be a major loser, Uncle Max is everything Wally longs to be . . . or so it appears. But Wally soon discovers the truth and learns who the real hero is in his life. (ISBN 0-8499-3876-7)

#13—My Life As a Blundering Ballerina

Wally agrees to switch places with Wall Street. Everyone is in on the act as the two try to survive seventy-two hours in each other's shoes and learn the importance of respecting other people. (ISBN 0-8499-4022-2)

#14—My Life As a Screaming Skydiver

Master of mayhem Wally turns a game of laser tag into international espionage. From the Swiss Alps to the African plains, Agent 00½th bumblingly employs such top-secret gizmos as rocket-powered toilet paper, exploding dental floss, and the ever-popular transformer tacos to stop the dreaded and super secret . . . Giggle Gun. (ISBN 0-8499-4023-0)

#15—My Life As a Human Hairball

When Wally and Wall Street visit a local laboratory, they are accidentally miniaturized and swallowed by some unknown stranger. It is a race against the clock as they fly through various parts of the body in a desperate search for a way out while learning how wonderfully we're made. (ISBN 0-8499-4024-9)

#16—My Life As a Walrus Whoopee Cushion

Wally and his buddies, Opera and Wall Street, win the Gazillion Dollar Lotto! Everything is great, until they realize they lost the ticket at the zoo! Add some bungling bad guys, a zoo break-in, the release of all the animals, a SWAT team or two . . . and you have the usual McDoogle mayhem as Wally learns the dangers of greed. (ISBN 0-8499-4025-7)

#17—My Life As a Mixed-Up Millennium Bug

When Wally accidentally fries the circuits of Ol' Betsy, his beloved laptop computer, suddenly whatever he types turns into reality! At 11:59, New Year's Eve, Wally tries retyping the truth into his computer—which shorts out every other computer in the world. By midnight, the entire universe has credited Wally's mishap to the MILLENNIUM BUG! Panic, chaos, and hilarity start the new century, thanks to our beloved boy blunder. (ISBN 0-8499-4026-5)

#18—My Life As a Beat-Up Basketball Backboard

Ricko Slicko's Advertising Agency claims that they can turn the dorkiest human in the world into the most popular. And who better to prove this than our boy blunder, Wally McDoogle! Soon he has his own TV series and fans wearing glasses just like his. But when he tries to be a star athlete for his school basketball team, Wally finally learns that being popular isn't all it's cut out to be. (ISBN 0-8499-4027-3)

#19—My Life As a Cowboy Cowpie

Once again our part-time hero and full-time walking disaster area finds himself smack-dab in another misadventure. This time it's full of dude-ranch disasters, bungling broncobusters, and the world's biggest cow—well, let's just say it's not a pretty picture (or a pleasant-smelling one). Through it all, Wally learns the dangers of seeking revenge. (ISBN 0-8499-5990-X)

#20—My Life As Invisible Intestines

When Wally becomes invisible, he can do whatever he wants, like humiliating bullies, or helping the local football team win. But the fun is short-lived when everyone from a crazy ghostbuster to the *59 1/2 Minutes* TV show to the neighbor's new dog begin pursuing him. Soon Wally is stumbling and through another incredible disaster . . . until he finally learns that cheating and taking shortcuts in life are not all they're cracked up to be and that honesty really is the best policy. (ISBN 0-8499-5991-8)